English
is Fun

跟著TE〔
快速學

鐘

美語輕鬆學
★ ★ ★

輕/鬆/學/會

美語會話

TED名師傳授566學美語的方法

5原則・6行動・6個月，快速學會新語言

附
MP3

蘇盈盈 —— 著

哈福

前言

如何輕鬆學會說美語

　　什麼是學語言最好、最有效的方法，相信每個人的答案和經驗都不一樣。因為每個人的學習習慣並不盡相同，吸收能力也不一樣。有些人喜歡到當地學習、有些人喜歡啃文法書、有些人喜歡嘗試新奇獨特的方法，體驗與眾不同的學習方式。其實不管哪一種方法，自己吸收的效果好，就是最有效的學習方式。

　　外語名師在 **TED** 的演講中提到：1000 句會話，就含蓋了 85% 老外每天說的話了。5 個原則、6 個動作，6 個月就能學會一種新的語言，在這裡特別推薦給有心想學好外語的讀者。

5 個原則：

　　1. 專注學習；2. 當溝通工具；3. 交流聊天；4. 訓練大腦接受新語言的聲調；5. 保持好心情，會很快學好新語言。

6 個動作：

　　1. 學 1000 個核心單詞就夠了；2. 大量聽、隨時聽；3. 大量學，無限擴充和聯想，你就可以脫口說 1000 句會話；4. 理解意思；5. 模仿；6. 左右腦圖像記憶，記得久。

　　我常常說，要學好一種語言，最有效的方法就是，聽講該種語言的人怎麼說，我們就跟著怎麼說，隨時隨地，想辦法聽你想要學的那種語言人家是怎麼說的？

　　要學該種語言時，就不要去想中文，最忌諱的是，用中文去翻譯成外國語言，這樣講出來的話，肯定是「雞同鴨講」，常常會搞

的對方一頭霧水,不知道到你在說什麼,更糟的是,對方誤解你的意思,如果只是平常聊天那還沒關係,如果是談正事,當對方誤解你的意思時,事情可能就搞砸了。

筆者曾看過一本書,該書裡教 garbage food,就是指「一些沒有營養的零食」,也叫做「垃圾食物」,如果,你真的這樣學了,當你看到外國朋友在吃零食時,你說他在吃 garbage food,對方肯定對你很不滿意。為什麼會有 garbage food 這種英語出現呢,那就是用中文去翻譯成英語。

要知道「零食」的英語是 junk food,junk 這個字含有「沒用的、垃圾」的意思,當然 junk food 可以翻譯成「垃圾食物」,但是「垃圾食物」絕不能說成 garbage food。garbage 這個字是「真正的垃圾」的意思,是那些人家丟掉不用的,骯髒的垃圾。但是 junk 是「沒有用」的意思,所有,美國人說零食是 junk food,是說吃零食沒有營養。但是零食絕不可能是 garbage food,因為 garbage 是垃圾,是不能吃的。

美國人怎麼說,我們就跟著怎麼說

平常聊天說話,可不是考試或是問答題,聊天說話應該是輕鬆的、你一句我一句,什麼都可以說,跟老美聊天時,該說甚麼話呢?

本書為您提供很多「虛擬實境」,將最生活化的美語情境,呈現在你的面前,你將發現說英語原來是這麼輕鬆、簡單。

我已經再三強調,要學美語,就是跟著美國人學,他們怎麼說,我們就跟著怎麼說。

要想很輕鬆地學會一口流利的美語,最好的方法是跟著本書由美國專業播音員所錄製的語言 MP3 唸,而且是大聲地唸,唸久了,這些句子自然成了你的語言,不知不覺,淘淘不絕。

前言 如何輕鬆學會說美語 2

Chapter 1 Going Shopping （去購物）

Chapter 2 Feelings （用英語表達感情）

Chapter **3** Things that people do（事件）

Chapter 1

Going Shopping

（去購物）

Going to the store

（去商店）

 實用句型

I'm going shopping.	我要去購物。
Do you need anything?	你需要什麼東西嗎？
Can I pick up something for you at the store?	我到了商店，要替你買什麼東西嗎？
Is there anything you want me to add to the list?	有沒有什麼東西，你要我加到購物單上？
He wants some oranges.	他要一些柳丁。
What else should I get to go with dinner?	還需要我買什麼東西做晚餐嗎？

Do you want to come along?	你要不要一起來？

A: I'm going shopping.

Do you want to come along?

（我要去購物，你要一起來嗎？）

B: I need to but I'm too busy right now.

（我需要去，但是我現在很忙。）

A: Is there anything you want me to pick up for you?

（你要我幫你買什麼東西嗎？）

B: Yes. I'd like some oranges if you don't mind.

（好，如果你不介意的話，請幫我買一些柳丁。）

開口說英語二

A: Are you going shopping today?

（你今天要去購物嗎？）

B: I sure am.

I'm making out my list right now.

（（是的，我現在在寫購物單。）

A: Could you put bread on the list?

（你可以把麵包放到購物單上嗎？）

B: No problem.

Is there anything else you want me to add?

（沒問題，你還要加什麼東西嗎？）

A: No, that should do it.

（沒有，我只要麵包。）

B: Okay then. I'm off to the store.

（好的，我要去商店了。）

單字

store [stor]	名	商店
add [æd]		加
list [lɪst]		購物單
busy [ˈbɪzɪ]		忙的
mind [maɪnd]	動	介意
problem [ˈprɑbləm]		問題
else [ɛls]		其他的

Buying Clothes

（買衣服）

I need some new clothes.	我需要一些新衣服。
He needs some new jeans.	他需要一些新的牛仔褲。
What size does she wear?	她穿幾號的？
There's a great sale at Sears.	席爾斯百貨公司有個大拍賣。
I have to buy a new suit for work.	我需要買一件上班的套裝。
It's time to buy school clothes again.	該是買上學的衣服的時候了。

A: What are you doing today?

（你今天要做什麼？）

B: I need some new clothes so I'm going shopping.

（我需要一些衣服，所以我要去購物。）

A: What are you going to buy?

（你要買什麼？）

B: I need a new suit for work and some new shoes.

（我需要一件上班的套裝，還要幾雙新鞋子。）

A: My kids need some new clothes for school.

（我的小孩需要上學的新衣服。）

B: Then why don't you come with me?
You might find something for them.

（那你何不跟我一起去？你可能可以找到一些他們需要的東西。）

 開口說英語二

A: Jenny needs a new pair of jeans.

（珍妮需要一件新的牛仔褲。）

B: What size does she wear?

（她穿幾號的？）

A: I think she wears a four.

（我想是四號。）

B: They are having a great sale at Sears.

（席爾斯百貨公司在大拍賣。）

A: Terrific.

（那可真棒。）

I think I'll check it out.

（我想我會去看看。）

 單字

clothes [kloðz]		衣物
jeans [dʒinz]		牛仔褲
size [saɪz]		大小；尺碼
wear [wɛr]		動 穿；戴
sale [sel]		拍賣
suit [sut]		西裝；一套衣服
terrific [təˈrɪfɪk]		真棒

Buying Shoes

（買鞋子）

實用句型

MP3-04

I'm looking for a pair of sneakers.	我想買一雙布鞋。
Are these real leather?	這些是真皮的嗎？
What size do those come in?	那雙鞋你們有哪些尺寸？
Do you have these in a seven?	這雙鞋你們有七號嗎？
I need some new shoes.	我需要一些新鞋子。
The shoe store is having a sale.	那家鞋店在拍賣。

She needs some pumps to go with her dress.	她需要幾雙皮鞋配她的洋裝。
These come in several colors.	這雙鞋有好幾種顏色。
I'm not sure I like that style.	我不確定我喜歡這種樣式。

 開口說英語一

A: Can I help you?

（需要我幫忙嗎？）

B: Yes, I'm looking for a pair of boots.

（是的，我要買一雙馬靴。）

A: What do you think of these?

（這雙你覺得怎麼樣？）

B: I'm not sure I like that style.

（我不確定我喜歡那個樣式。）

Do you have anything else?

（你有沒有其它的？）

A: We have these.

（我們還有這個樣式。）

B: I like those.

（我喜歡那雙。）

I'll take them in a size eight please.

（請給我八號的。）

開口說英語二

A: My daughter needs a pair of pumps to match her new dress.

（我女兒需要一雙皮鞋配她的新洋裝。）

B: This style here comes in several colors.

（這邊這個樣式有好幾種顏色。）

A: I like these red ones.

Do they come in a five?

（我喜歡紅色的，它們有五號嗎？）

B: Yes, they do. Would you like a pair of them? They are on sale for twenty-five dollars.

（有，你要一雙嗎？這個樣式正在打折拍賣，只要二十五元。）

A: Are they real leather?

（它們是真皮的嗎？）

B: Yes. They certainly are.

（是的，是真皮的。）

A: Okay, We'll take them.

（好的，那我買了。）

單字

sneaker	[ˈsnikɚ]	布鞋
leather	[ˈlɛðɚ]	皮革
pump	[pʌmp]	（女士穿的，無鞋帶的）皮鞋
several	[ˈsɛvrəl]	幾個
style	[staɪl]	名 樣式；型式
boot	[but]	馬靴
match	[mætʃ]	動 相配
certainly	[ˈsɝtn̩lɪ]	當然

The Pet Store

（寵物店）

實用句型

I'm looking for a pet for my son.	我要替我兒子買隻寵物。
How much is that kitten?	那隻貓多少錢？
She'd like to buy some toys for her rat.	她要買一些玩具給她的寵物老鼠。
Can I put these fish in the same tank?	我可以把這些魚放在同一個水箱嗎？
Do you have anything cheaper?	你有沒有便宜一點的？

開口說英語一

A: I'm looking for a pet for my son.

（我要為我的兒子買一隻寵物。）

B: Does he like cats?

We have a lot of new kittens.

（他喜歡貓嗎？我們進了許多新的小貓。）

A: Let me see them.

How much is that gray one?

（讓我看看，灰色的那隻多少錢？）

B: Seventy-five dollars.

（七十五塊。）

A: Okay. I think I'll take him.

（好的，我買了。）

A: What a beautiful fish.

（好漂亮的魚。）

B: Are you thinking of buying him?

（你要買嗎？）

A: Yes, but I already have several fish at home. Can I put him in the tank with the others?

（是的，但是我家裡已經有好幾隻魚，我可以把這隻跟其他的放在同一個水箱嗎？）

B: No, he will fight with them.

He has to have a tank all to himself.

（不行，他會跟他們打架，他必須有他自己的水箱。）

 單字

pet [pɛt]		寵物
kitten ['kɪtn̩]		小貓
toy [tɔɪ]		玩具
rat [ræt]		老鼠
tank [tæŋk]		水槽
cheaper ['tʃipɚ]		較便宜的
gray [gre]		灰色的
beautiful ['bjutəfəl]	名	美麗的；漂亮的
already [ɔl'rɛdɪ]	副	已經
fight [faɪt]		爭吵
himself ['hɪmsɛlf]		他自己

At the Bookstore

（在書店）

實用句型

MP3-06

I'm looking for a book by Steven King.	我在找史蒂芬金寫的書。
I need a book for school.	我學校裡需要一本書。
Do you have any books about dragons?	你們有沒有關於龍的書？
Where would books for Classical Literature be located?	『古典文學』的書會放在那裡？
Do you carry "A Tale of Two Cities"?	你們有沒有賣「雙城記」？

 開口說英語一

A: Can I help you find something?

（你需要我幫忙嗎？）

B: Yes, I'm looking for a book by Dickens. I'm not sure what it's called.

（是的，我在找狄根斯寫的書，我不太知道書名叫什麼。）

A: His books will be in the fiction section over there. They are listed in alphabetical order using the author's name.

（他的書放在那邊的小說類，書是以作者的名字按字母排列。）

B: If I don't find it, can I order it?

（如果我找不到，我可不可以訂購？）

A: Sure, I can do that for you. If you need anything else, just let me know.

（可以，我們可以替你訂購，如果你需要其他的東西，跟我說一聲。）

B: Okay, thanks for your help.

（好的，謝謝你的幫忙。）

開口說英語二

A: Excuse me.
Do you carry Silver Dragons?

（對不起，你們有「銀龍」這本書嗎？）

B: I'm not sure but I can look it up for you.

（我不太確定，但是我可以幫你找找看。）

A: Thank you. It's a children's book.

（謝謝，那是一本小孩子的書。）

B: I'm sorry. We don't have that title. But we do have several other books about dragons.

（對不起，我們沒有那本書，但是我們有好幾本有關龍的書。）

A: Could you show me where to find them?

（你可以告訴我那些書放哪裡嗎？）

B: Sure. Right this way.

（可以，這邊走。）

dragon [ˈdrægən]		龍
located [loˈketɪd]	位於（locate的過去分詞）	
carry [ˈkærɪ]		（商店）售貨
fiction [ˈfɪkʃən]		名 小說

section [ˈsɛkʃən]		（零售店的）部門
list [lɪst]		動 排列
author [ˈɔθɚ]		名 作者；作家
alphabetical [ælfəˈbɛtɪl]		按照字母的
title [ˈtaɪtl̩]		名 書名
show [ʃo]		展示；給(某人)看

Buying Music

（買音樂光碟）

 實用句型

MP3-07

I'm looking for a CD.	我要買一張音樂光碟。
Do you have anything by The Backstreet Boys?	你們有沒有任何「新好男孩」的音樂？
We have the newest release.	我們有最近剛推出的。
Do you want a cassette or a CD?	你要卡帶還是光碟？
Where could I find Black and Blue ?	「藍與黑」的唱片放在那裡？

開口說英語一

A: Do you have any Classical CD's?

（你們有古典音樂光碟嗎？）

B: We sure do. What are you looking for?

（我們有，你在找什麼？）

A: I'm looking for a Mozart CD.

（我在找莫札特的音樂光碟。）

B: We have several different ones.

If you'd like, I can play one for you.

（我們有好幾個不同的，如果你要的話，我可以放一張給你聽。）

開口說英語二

A: Can I help you?

（需要我幫忙嗎？）

B: Yeah, I'm looking for The Beatles.

（我在找「披頭四」的音樂。）

A: We have their latest release.
It just came in today.

（我們有他們最新發行的，今天剛進來。）

B: Great, I'll take it.

（很好，我買了。）

A: Would you like a cassette or CD?

（你要卡帶還是光碟？）

B: A CD will be fine, thank you.

（我買光碟好了，謝謝你。）

單字

release	[rɪˈlis]	發行
cassette	[kəsɛt]	卡帶
different	[ˈdɪfərənt]	形 不同的

At the Gift Shop

（禮品店）

實用句型

MP3-08

I'm looking for a gift for my sister.	我要買一個禮物給我妹妹。
Which one do you recommend?	你建議哪一個？
My mother collects bells.	我的母親收集鈴鐺。
This would be great for my father.	這個送給我父親最棒。
Do you have anything cheaper?	你們有沒有便宜一點的？
Does that one come in red?	那一個有紅色的嗎？

開口說英語一

A: I'm looking for a gift for my mother. It's her birthday and I want to get her something nice.

（我要買一個禮物給我母親，她的生日到了，我要買一件好禮物給她。）

B: We have this set of crystal dishes for only $350.00

（我們有一套水晶碟子，只要三百五十元。）

A: That's a little more than I have. Do you have anything cheaper?

（這個價錢超出我的預算，你們有沒有便宜一點的東西？）

B: What about this bracelet? It's only $200.00

（這一隻手鐲怎麼樣？，只要兩百元。）

A: That's really pretty.
I think she'd like it a lot.

（這手鐲很漂亮。，我想她會喜歡。）

開口說英語二

A: Can I help you with anything?

（你需要我幫什麼忙嗎？）

B: I'm looking for a gift for my friend.
He collects dragons and bats.

（我要找一個禮物給我朋友，他收集龍和蝙蝠。）

A: We don't have any bats but we do have
some dragons.

（我們沒有蝙蝠，但是我們有一些龍。）

B: That one is nice but I'm not sure about
the color.

（那個不錯，但是顏色我不是很喜歡。）

A: It also comes in red and green.

（那個也有紅色和綠色的。）

B: I think he'd really like the green one.
Could you please gift wrap it for me?

（我想他會喜歡綠色的，你可以把它包成禮物嗎？）

單字

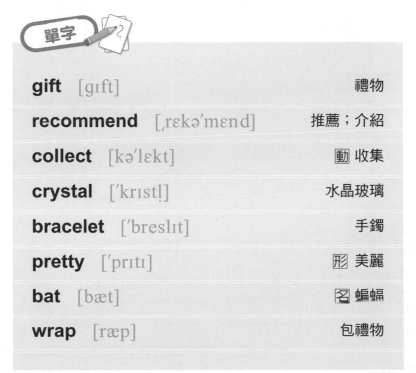

gift [gɪft]		禮物
recommend [ˌrɛkə'mɛnd]		推薦；介紹
collect [kə'lɛkt]	動	收集
crystal ['krɪstl̩]		水晶玻璃
bracelet ['breslɪt]		手鐲
pretty ['prɪtɪ]	形	美麗
bat [bæt]	名	蝙蝠
wrap [ræp]		包禮物

MP3-09

My wife likes diamonds a lot.	我太太很喜歡鑽石。
I'd really like to get her a ruby.	我想為她買個紅寶石。
I just want something simple.	我想買樣式簡單一點的。
Do you carry earrings?	你們有耳環嗎？
What size does he wear?	他戴幾號的？

A: I want to buy my father a ring.

（我想買一個戒指給我父親。）

B: Are you looking for something with stones in it?

（你要買鑲石頭的嗎？）

A: Actually, I just want something simple.

（事實上，我只想買樣式簡單一點的。）

B: We have some very nice bands over here.

（我們有一些不錯的指環。）

A: Can I get this sized if it doesn't fit him? He's a very big man and this seems small.

（如果這個他戴起來不合的話，我可以拿來修改尺寸嗎？他人蠻高大的，這個看起來小小的。）

B: If it doesn't fit him, don't worry.

Bring it back and we'll size it for free.

（如果不合，別擔心，拿回來，我們會免費修改大小。）

 開口說英語二

A: I'm looking for a diamond ring for my wife.

I'd also like to get her a ruby, too.

（我要買一個鑽石戒指給我太太，也想買一個紅寶石給她。）

B: We have these diamond and ruby sets.

（我們有這些鑽石和紅寶石組合。）

A: They look big.

She has very small fingers.

（他們看起來很大，她的手指頭很小。）

B: Maybe you should get her a bracelet instead.

（或許你應該買個手鐲給她。）

A: That sounds like an idea.
Let's see what you've got.

（那倒是個好主意，讓我看看你們有什麼？）

 單字

diamond [ˈdaɪəmənd]		鑽石
ruby [ˈrubɪ]		紅寶石
simple [ˈsɪmpl̩]		簡單的
earrings [ˈɪrɪŋz]		名 耳環
	（多用複數形，表示一對）	
ring [rɪŋ]		戒指
actually [ˈæktʃʊəlɪ]		副 實際上；事實上
band [bænd]		名 戒子

fit [fɪt]		合適
worry [ˈwɝɪ]		動 憂慮；擔心
free [fri]		形 免費的
finger [ˈfɪŋgɚ]		手指
instead [ɪnˈstɛd]		不是...而是

Unit 9

Buying Make-up

（買化妝品）

What do you think? Is this my color?	你看怎麼樣？這個顏色適合嗎？
That shade is very flattering on you.	這個色調你用起來蠻出色的。
You look great.	你看起來很漂亮。
I love that lipstick.	我喜歡那支口紅。
Can I get a polish to match?	你們有可以相配的亮光口紅嗎？
That shade goes perfect with your dress.	那個色調跟你的洋裝很相配。
My skin is too dry.	我的皮膚很乾燥。

開口說英語一

A: What do you think, Mary?
Is this my color?
（瑪麗，你認為怎麼樣？這個顏色適合我嗎？）

B: That shade goes perfect with your dress.
（那個顏色跟你的洋裝很相配。）

A: Really? I think I'll buy it.
（真的？我想我會買。）

B: Be sure to get a polish to match.
（記得買一支亮光口紅來搭配。）

開口說英語二

A: What do you think?

（你認為怎麼樣？）

B: I love that lipstick.

That shade is very flattering, too.

（我喜歡那支口紅，那顏色令你看起來更好看。）

A: Thanks but I'm still having trouble finding a foundation.

My skin is too dry and it keeps peeling off.

（謝謝你，但是我仍然找不到適合的粉底，我的皮膚太乾燥，一直會脫皮。）

B: Why don't you try a foundation with moisturizer? It's made for people with very dry skin.

（你何不試試有滋潤液的粉底？那是特地為乾燥皮膚的人做的。）

單字

shade	[ʃed]	色調
flatter	[flætɚ]	使優點顯得突出
lipstick	[ˈlɪpstɪk]	唇膏
polish	[ˈpɑlɪʃ]	亮光唇膏
perfect	[ˈpɝfɪkt]	完美的
dry	[draɪ]	名 乾的
skin	[skɪn]	皮膚
foundation	[faʊnˈdeʃən]	粉底
peel	[pil]	剝落
moisturizer	[ˈmɔɪstʃəˌraɪzɚ]	乳液

Buying School Supplies

（買學校用品）

實用句型

MP3-11

Anne needs some more paper.	安妮需要更多的紙。
How many notebooks do you need?	你需要幾本筆記本？
Are there any pens and pencils left?	還有鋼筆或鉛筆剩下嗎？
Don't forget to get scissors and glue.	別忘了買剪刀和漿糊。
I need a new ruler.	我需要一支新的尺。
I could use a new box of crayons.	一盒新的粉筆會很好。

開口說英語一

A: I've got to buy school supplies for the kids.

（我需要替孩子們買文具。）

B: What do they need?

（他們需要什麼？）

A: Anne needs some paper and Jimmy needs a new pen.

（安妮需要更多的紙，吉米需要一支新的筆。）

B: Make sure they have notebooks while you're out.

（你出去買時，要確定他們有筆記本。）

A: Mary, do you need a notebook for class?

（瑪麗，你學校裡需要筆記本嗎？）

B: No. I still have two notebooks.

（不需要，我還有兩本筆記本。）

A: Okay, I've got the scissors and the glue. Is there anything else you need?

（好的，我已經買了剪刀和漿糊，你還需要其他什麼嗎？）

B: I could use a new ruler and some map pencils.

（一支新的尺和色筆會很好。）

A: That's fine.

（好的。）

單字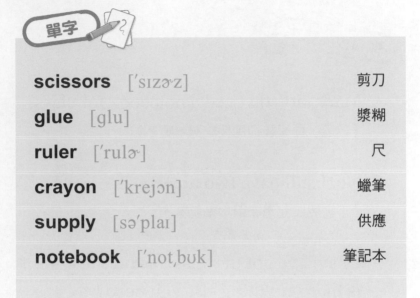

scissors [ˈsɪzɚz]		剪刀
glue [glu]		漿糊
ruler [ˈrulɚ]		尺
crayon [ˈkrejɔn]		蠟筆
supply [səˈplaɪ]		供應
notebook [ˈnotˌbʊk]		筆記本

Buying Toys

（買玩具）

實用句型

MP3-12

What kind of toys would an eight-year-old like?	八歲小孩喜歡什麼玩具？
Do you carry toy trains?	你們有玩具火車嗎？
I'm looking for some Star Wars figures.	我在找「星際大戰」的人物造型玩具。
My niece wants a Barbie.	我姪女要一個芭比娃娃。
How much is that toy train?	那個玩具火車多少錢？
Does this take batteries?	這個玩具需要電池嗎？
Is this something he can play with by himself?	這個玩具他可以自己一個人玩嗎？

開口說英語一

A: Maybe you can help me.

What kind of toys would a nine-year-old boy like?

（或許你可以幫我的忙？一個九歲的小孩喜歡什麼？）

B: Some toy cars might be a good idea.

We have this remote control car for only $15.00.

（他們可能會喜歡玩具車，這個遙控車只要十五塊。）

A: That sounds good.

Does it take batteries?

（好像不錯，需要電池嗎？）

B: It takes three AA's.

We have some of those up front.

（需要三個ＡＡ的電池，我們店門口有擺一些ＡＡ的電池。）

A: Do you carry Star Wars toys?

（你們有沒有「星際大戰」的玩具？）

B: We sure do. What are you looking for?

（我們有，你在找什麼？）

A: I don't want an action figure.

I was thinking of a game.

（我不喜歡造型人物，我想買遊戲。）

A: This game is for ages 10 and up.

（這個遊戲是給十歲以上的小孩玩。）

B: How many people does it take to play it?

（需要幾個人才能玩？）

A: It is designed for two to four players.

（它是設計給兩個到四個人玩。）

B: I'll take it.

（我買了。）

單字

kind	[kaɪnd]	種類
figure	['fɪgjɚ]	人物
niece	[nis]	姪女
battery	['bætərɪ]	電瓶；電池
idea	[aɪ'dɪə]	主意
remote	[rɪ'mot]	图 遙控器
control	[kən'trol]	控制
front	[frʌnt]	前面
design	[dɪ'zaɪn]	設計

Unit 12

Buying Furniture

（買家具）

I'm interested in finding a new bed.	我想買一個新的床。
My wife wants a new living room suite.	我太太想要一套新的客廳家具組。
I'd like to see your dining room sets.	我想要看看你們的餐廳家具組。
Does this mattress come with a guarantee?	這個床墊有附保證嗎？
Can you deliver this?	你們會運送過來嗎？
How much extra is the additional chair?	另加一張椅子要加多少錢？
Does this come in any other color?	這個有其他的顏色嗎？
I think I like the blue one the best.	我想我最喜歡藍色那個。

開口說英語一

A: I'm looking for a new living room suite.

（我想要買一組新的客廳家具。）

B: Is there anything in particular you're after?

（你特別要買什麼嗎？）

A: No, I'm just getting some ideas.

（沒有，我還在到處看看。）

B: This one comes with a couch, a loveseat, and three tables.
For only $250 more we'll throw in this chair.

（這組包括一個沙發椅，一個雙人沙發和三張桌子，再加個兩百五十元，我們可以再給你這張椅子。）

開口說英語二

A: I'd like some information on this dinette set.

（我想多知道這套餐廳家具。）

B: Certainly.

What would you like to know?

（好的，你想知道什麼？）

A: Does it come in any other color besides green?

（除了綠色之外，它們還有什麼其他的顏色嗎？）

B: We have it in red and purple also.

（還有紅色和紫色。）

A: Is the table included in the price?

（這個價錢包括這張桌子嗎？）

B: Yes, you get all five pieces.

（是的，你可以買到全部五樣。）

單字

suite [swit]		一套家具
mattress ['mætrɪs]		床墊
guarantee [ˌgærən'ti]		保證
deliver [dɪ'lɪvɚ]	動	遞送；送貨
extra ['ɛkstrə]		額外的；多餘的
additional [ə'dɪʃənəl]		額外的；另外的
particular [pɚ'tɪkjələ]	形	特別的；特定的
loveseat ['lʌsit]		兩人座沙發椅
couch [kaʊtʃ]		沙發椅
information [ˌɪnfɚ'meʃən]		資料；資訊
besides [bɪ'saɪdz]	副	除此以外
include [ɪn'klud]		包括

Buying Household Supplies

（買家用物品）

Do we need any soap?	我們需要肥皂嗎？
Pick up some detergent while you're at the store.	你到商店時，買一些洗碗精。
We're almost out of toilet paper.	我們的衛生紙快沒有了。
I think we're going to need some napkins.	我想我們需要一些紙巾。
I could use a new mop.	買一隻新的拖把會很好。
How much toothpaste do we have left?	我們還剩下多少牙膏？

開口說英語一

A: How much soap do we have left?

（我們還剩下多少肥皂？）

B: We still have enough for a couple of washes.

（我們還有足夠洗幾次。）

A: Can you think of anything we might need?

（你想一想我們還需要什麼？）

B: We could probably use some more toothpaste.

（買一些牙膏好了。）

A: I'm going to the store to get some detergent.

（我要到店裡去買一些洗碗精。）

B: Could you pick up a mop and a broom while you're there.

（你到店裡時，請你買一隻拖把和一隻掃帚。）

A: Sure. How are we on toilet paper?

（好的，我們的衛生紙還有嗎？）

B: We're almost out and we need some tissues, too.

（我們衛生紙快用完了，我們也需要一些面紙。）

單字

soap	[sop]	名	肥皂
detergent	[dɪˈtɝdʒənt]		洗碗精
toilet paper			衛生紙
almost	[ˈɔl͵most]	副	幾乎
toothpaste	[ˈtuθpæst]		牙膏
mop	[mɑp]		拖把
napkin	[ˈnæpkɪn]		餐巾；紙巾
enough	[ɪˈnʌf]		足夠的
probably	[ˈprɑbəblɪ]		或許；可能的
broom	[brum]		掃帚
tissue	[ˈtɪʃʊ]		紙巾

Buying Video Games

（買電動玩具）

實用句型

I'm looking for a video game.	我想買一個電動玩具。
What kind of system do you have?	你們有什麼電動玩具的系統？
I need a video game for a nine-year-old boy.	我需要一個給九歲男孩的電動玩具。
This game has great graphics.	這個遊戲的圖像很好看。
How many people can play at once?	一次多少人可以玩？
Does this have more than one level?	這個遊戲多於一個關卡嗎？

This game even has a practice level.	這個遊戲有練習的關卡。
It is great for beginners.	對初學者很好。
Is your daughter an advanced player?	你的女兒玩的很高竿嗎？

開口說英語一

A: I'm looking for a video game.

（我在找一個電動玩具。）

B: What kind of system do you have?

（你有什麼系統？）

A: I have an N64 and a PlayStation.

（我有N64和PlayStation。）

B: Then you need to look at these right over here.

（那你需要看看這邊的電動玩具。）

A: How many people can play this game?

（多少人可以玩這個遊戲？）

B: It has a setting for one or two players.

（它可以一個到兩個人玩。）

A: Does it have more than one level?

（它有多於一個關卡嗎？）

B: It has sixteen levels.

Four of them are for beginners.

（它有十六個關卡，其中四個關卡是給初學者玩的。）

 單字

video game	電動玩具
system [ˈsɪstəm]	系統
graphics [ˈgræfɪks]	圖
level [ˈlɛvl̩]	關卡
beginner [bɪˈgɪnɚ]	初學者
advanced [ədˈvæst]	高級的
player [ˈpleɚ]	玩家；競賽者

Buying Gift Certificates

（買禮券）

I don't know what to get my aunt.	我不知道該買什麼給我的姨媽。
I'm thinking about buying him a gift certificate.	我想買禮券給他。
What is the amount of the gift certificate?	一張禮券面額多少？
Can she use the gift certificate for anything?	這張禮券她什麼都可以買嗎？
Which items can't be bought with a gift certificate?	那些物品不能用禮券買？

Are there any items not covered by the gift certificate?	有沒有哪些項目不能用禮券買？

A: I don't know what to get my aunt.

（我不知道該買什麼給我的姨媽。）

B: How about a gift certificate?

（你何不買一張禮券給她？）

A: Can she use it to buy anything in the store?

（她可以用禮券買店裡任何東西嗎？）

B: It covers everything up to the value on it.

（她可以購買不超過禮券金額的任何東西。）

A: How much are your gift certificates?

（你的禮券是多少錢？）

B: We have $25, $50, and $100 certificates.

（我們有二十五元的，五十元的，和一百元的禮券。）

A: What items aren't covered by the certificate?

（有哪些項目不能用禮券買？）

B: Everything in the store is covered.

（店裡的任何項目都可以用禮券買。）

A: Great. I need three $100 gift certificates.

（很好，我需要三張一百元的禮券。）

B: No problem. Here you are.

（好的，你的禮券在這裡。）

單字

certificate	[sɚˈtɪfəˌkɪt]	證書
gift certificate		禮券
item	[ˈaɪtəm]	貨品；項目

Buying a Car

（買車）

MP3-17

How does it run?	這部車開起來怎麼樣？
I'd like to test drive it.	我想要試開。
What is the asking price?	你要價多少？
Are you looking for a new car or a used one?	你要買新車還是舊車？
I need something dependable.	我需要可靠的車子。
How much mileage does it get?	這部車已開了多少哩？
Can I order it in green?	我可以訂購一部綠色的嗎？

A: I'm thinking about buying a car.

（我想買一部車子。）

B: Are you looking for a new car or a used one?

（你要買新車還是舊車？）

A: I'm not sure yet.

I need something dependable.

（我還不確定，我需要可靠的車子。）

B: I think I have the car for you.

（我想我有適合的車子給你。）

開口說英語二

A: So, what do you think of this car?

（你認為這部車子怎麼樣？）

B: It looks great. But how does it run?

（看起來很好，是開起來怎麼樣？）

A: It runs perfectly.

You won't find a better car.

（很好開，你找不到更好的車子。）

B: Maybe.

I'd like to test drive it before I decide.

（或許，我做決定之前要先試開。）

單字

drive [draɪv]		動 開車
test drive		試開
used [juzd]		使用過的；二手的
dependable [dɪˈpɛndəb!]		可靠的
mileage [ˈmaɪlɪdʒ]		里程
perfectly [ˈpɝfɪktlɪ]		無瑕疵的
decide [dɪˈsaɪd]		動 決定

Unit

17

Buying a New Home

（買新房子）

MP3-18

I'm in the market for a new house.	我在找新房子。
She's looking for a three-bedroom, two-bathroom house.	她在找一間三房兩衛的房子。
How much do you want down?	你頭款要多少？
I can give you $20,000.	我可以給你兩萬塊。
He needs something closer to his family.	他需要一間靠近他家人的房子。

開口說英語一

A: Lee's Realtors. How can I help you?
（這裡是李氏房地產公司，你需要什麼？）

B: I'm in the market for a new home.
（我在找新房子。）

A: Well, what exactly are you looking for?
（你在找什麼樣的房子？）

B: I don't know. I'm thinking about a four-bedroom, two-bathroom house.
（我不知道，我在考慮四房兩衛的房子。）

開口說英語二

A: How much are you asking down?

（頭款你們要求多少錢？）

B: We're asking $25,000. That will make the monthly payments $700.

（我們要兩萬五的頭款，這樣每個月的付款大約是七百元。）

A: I can give you $20,000 now and pay $850 a month.

（我可以現在給你兩萬塊，然後一個月付八百五十元。）

B: That sounds reasonable.

（聽起來蠻合理的。）

單字

market [ˈmɑrkɪt]		市場
bathroom [ˈbæθrum]	名	浴室
down [daʊn]		頭款
exactly [ɪgˈzæktlɪ]		確切的
payment [ˈpemənt]	名	付款
monthly [ˈmʌnθlɪ]		每月的
reasonable [ˈriznəbl̩]		合理的

Buying Tickets for Events

（買看活動的票）

I'd like to purchase two tickets to see Cats.	我要兩張票看音樂劇「貓」。
He wants to get tickets for the Friday showing.	他要買星期五表演的票。
What time do I have to be there to pick up my ticket?	我需要幾點到那裡拿我的票？
Are there any tickets still available?	還有票嗎？
She is trying to find tickets for the concert next week.	她在找下星期的音樂會的票。

Can I pay by phone if I have a credit card?	如果我有信用卡，我可以用電話付錢嗎？
Is there any way I can get six seats together?	有什麼辦法可以拿到六張票連在一起？
Can I get tickets at the door?	我可以在門口買票嗎？

開口說英語一

A: Did you hear that "Cats" is coming?

（你有沒有聽說音樂劇「貓」要來上演了？）

B: Really. I'd love to go. Are there any tickets still available?

（真的，我想去看，還有票嗎？）

A: There are still some left but they're selling out quick.

（還有剩下一些票，但是它們賣得很快。）

B: Then I'd better go get mine today.

（那我最好今天就去買票。）

開口說英語二

A: Do I need to buy my ballet tickets in advance?

（我需要預先買芭蕾舞的票嗎？）

B: You can or you can get them at the door.

（你可以預先購買，也可以在門口購買。）

A: How much are they if I buy them in advance?

（如果我預先購買，多少錢？）

B: They are $30 each if you buy them before the show. On the night of the show they will be $50.

（預先購買一張是三十元，表演當晚的票要五十元。）

purchase ['pɝtʃəs]		購買
ticket ['tɪkɪt]		票
available [ə'veləbl]		有得賣的；可得的
concert ['kɑnsɚt]		图 演奏會；音樂會
credit card		信用卡
together [tə'gɛðɚ]		一起
quick [kwɪk]		快的；迅速的
left [lɛft]		剩下的
ballet ['bæle]		芭蕾舞
show [ʃo]		表演

Buying Souvenirs

（買紀念品）

 實用句型

MP3-20

I need to get some souvenirs for my family.	我要買一些紀念品給我的家人。
Let's get T-shirts.	我們來買T恤。
She bought a coffee mug for her father.	她買了一個馬克杯給她父親。
My uncle collects key chains.	我叔叔收集鑰匙鍊。
My mother wants me to bring her a souvenir.	我母親要我替她買一個紀念品。

A: Are we through shopping?

（我們逛完了嗎？）

B: No, let's stop here. I want to get some souvenirs for my family.

（還沒，我們再到這家逛逛，我想買一些紀念品給我的家人。）

A: What are you going to get them?

（你想買什麼給他們？）

B: They've never been to Italy before. I want to buy them all a shirt or something.

（他們沒到過義大利，我想給他們買一件襯衫或是其他什麼東西。）

開口說英語二

A: Thanks for bringing me to this concert.
This is one of my favorite bands.

（謝謝你帶我來音樂會，這是我最喜歡的樂團之一。）

B: Would you like a souvenir?
You could get a shirt.

（你要買一個紀念品嗎？你可以買一件襯衫。）

A: I'd love a shirt.
Are you getting one, too?

（我喜歡襯衫。你也要買一件嗎？）

B: No, I think I'll get a poster instead.

（不，我想我要買一張海報。）

單字

souvenir [ˌsuvəˈnɪr]		紀念品
mug [mʌg]		馬克杯
key chain		鑰匙鍊
through [θru]		完成的；結束的
shirt [ʃɝt]		襯衫
favorite [ˈfevərɪt]		最喜歡的
band [bænd]		名 樂隊
poster [ˈpostɚ]		海報

Feelings

（用英語表達感情）

Feeling Embarrassed

（覺得難堪）

MP3-21

I was so embarrassed.	我覺得很難堪。
I wanted to crawl under my desk and hide.	我真希望爬到桌子底下藏起來。
I've never felt so ashamed.	我沒有這麼難堪過。
It was humiliating.	真是令人難為情。
I've never been so embarrassed.	我從沒有這麼難堪過。
I felt like such a dork.	我覺得好像個笨蛋一樣。
I felt so stupid.	我覺得我好笨。

開口說英語一

A: I'm so embarrassed.

（我好難堪。）

B: What happened?

（什麼事？）

A: I accidentally called my teacher Mom.

（我不小心叫我的老師「媽」。）

B: How humiliating!

（好令人難堪啊。）

A: No wonder you're so red.

（難過你臉都紅了。）

開口說英語二

A: You look unhappy. What's wrong?

（你看起來很不快樂，怎麼啦？）

B: I've never been so ashamed in my life.

（我一生中從沒有這麼難堪過。）

A: Well, what happened?

（發生了什麼事？）

B: John yelled at me in front of the entire school. I felt like such a dork.

（約翰在整個學校面前對我吼叫，我覺得好像呆子一樣。）

A: I don't blame you for being embarrassed. That was a terrible thing for him to do.

（我不怪你那麼難堪，他這麼做真是過份。）

embarrassed [ɪmˈbærəst] 難為情的；難堪的

crawl [krɔwl] 爬

hide [haɪd] 隱藏

humiliating [hjuˈmɪlɪetɪŋ] 難為情的

dork [dɔrk] 呆子

accidentally [ˌæksəˈdɛntlɪ] 副 偶然地；意外地

ashamed [əˈʃemd] 感到羞恥的

blame [blem] 歸罪於

terrible [ˈtɛrəbl̩] 差勁的

Unit 2

Showing Excitement

（感到興奮）

MP3-22

That's amazing!	真不可思議。
How wonderful!	好棒。
What a spectacular idea.	真是好主意。
Most excellent!	真棒。
I can't wait!	我等不及。
Awesome!	好棒。

A: Look what I got today.

（你看我今天得到什麼。）

B: What is it?

（那是什麼？）

A: It's the newest video game system around.

（這是最新的電動玩具系統。）

B: That's awesome!
Have you played it yet?

（真棒，你玩了嗎？）

A: I thought we'd play after supper tonight.

（我想我們今晚晚餐之後再玩。）

B: I can't wait. Let's play it now.

（我等不及了，我們現在玩。）

A: We are going to see Phantom of the Opera.

（我們要去看『歌劇魅影』。）

B: How wonderful!
I've always wanted to see that.

（好棒，我一直想去看。）

A: I've got an extra ticket if you'd like to go.

（如果你想去，我有多一張票。）

B: Oh, thank you. I can't wait!

（謝謝，我等不及去看。）

Chapter 2 用英語表達感情

amazing [əˈmezɪŋ]		形 令人驚嘆的
wonderful [ˈwʌndɚfəl]		
		好棒的；絕妙的；好極了
spectacular [spɛkˈtækjəlɚ]		絕妙的
excellent [ˈɛksələnt]		很棒的
awesome [ˈɔsəm]		（口語）很棒的
extra [ˈɛkstrə]		額外的；多餘的

95

Being Nervous

（緊張）

I'm so nervous.	我好緊張。
I've got butterflies in my stomach.	我緊張的直想吐。
He was shaking with nervousness.	他緊張的直發抖。
Were you nervous?	你緊張嗎？
She'd never been so nervous before.	她以前從沒有這麼緊張過？

A: How did the audition go?

（試演會進行得怎麼樣？）

B: I think it went well.

（我想進行得很順利。）

A: Were you nervous?

（你緊張嗎？）

B: Yes, but I tried to focus on the music.

（是的，但是我盡量專注於音樂上。）

A: What do you think about Mary?

（你認為瑪麗怎麼樣？）

B: I don't know. She makes me nervous.

（我不知道，她令我很緊張。）

A: What do you mean?

（你是什麼意思？）

B: I get butterflies in my stomach whenever I see her.

（每一次我看到她，我就緊張的直發抖。）

A: I think you like her.

（我想你是喜歡她。）

B: No, I don't!

（沒有。）

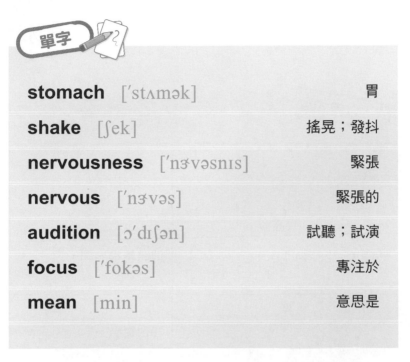

單字

stomach [ˈstʌmək]		胃
shake [ʃek]		搖晃；發抖
nervousness [ˈnɝvəsnɪs]		緊張
nervous [ˈnɝvəs]		緊張的
audition [ɔˈdɪʃən]		試聽；試演
focus [ˈfokəs]		專注於
mean [min]		意思是

實用句型

She was thrilled.	她開心極了。
He'll be tickled pink.	他將會很高興。
I love it!	我很喜歡。
How wonderful!	好棒。
It's the best!	那是最好的。

開口說英語一

A: Surprise! Here is your birthday gift.

（讓你驚喜一下！這是你的生日禮物。）

B: Oh, I love it! It's the most beautiful ring I've ever seen.

（噢，我很喜歡，這是我看過最漂亮的戒指。）

A: You really like it?

（你真的喜歡？）

B: Of course I like it.

（我當然喜歡。）

開口說英語二

A: What are you going to get John for graduation?

（你要給約翰什麼畢業禮物？）

B: I'm going to take him to Europe for two weeks.

（我要帶他去歐洲兩個星期。）

A: He'll be very happy. He's always wanted to go to Europe.

（他一定會很高興，他一直想去歐洲。）

B: I know. I can't wait to tell him.

（我知道，我等不及要告訴他。）

thrilled	[θrɪld]	高興極了
tickle	[ˈtɪkl̩]	呵…癢
surprise	[sɚˈpraɪz]	驚奇；驚喜
graduation	[ˌɡrædʒʊˈeʃən]	畢業
always	[ˈɔlwez]	總是

Being Angry

（生氣）

 實用句型

MP3-25

I can't stand it.	我受不了。
Can you believe it?	你會相信嗎？
The nerve of him!	他膽子真大。
He's really mad.	他真的很生氣。
She's going to lose it.	她會發脾氣。

開口說英語一

A: How was work today?

（今天上班怎麼樣？）

B: It was awful. My boss always picks on me. And today, he accused me of lying to him.

（真糟，我的上司總是找我麻煩，今天，他竟然指控我說謊騙他。）

A: What a jerk!

（真是無用的人。）

B: I know.

I thought I was going to lose it.

（我知道，我差點就跟他翻臉。）

A: So what did you do?

（那你怎麼辦？）

B: I decided to have a talk with his supervisor.

（我決定跟他的上司談一談。）

開口說英語二

A: Can you believe Jenny stole my necklace?

（你會相信珍妮竟然偷我的項鍊嗎？）

B: How do you know?

（你怎麼知道是她偷的？）

A: I saw her wearing it.

（我看到她戴著。）

B: Boy, I bet you were mad.

（天啊，我相信你一定很生氣。）

A: Can you believe the nerve of her?

（你相信她竟會這麼大膽嗎？）

B: I know. I couldn't stand it if my friend stole from me.

（我知道，我受不了我的朋友偷我的東西。）

 單字

stand [stænd]		動 忍受
nerve [nɝv]		神經
really [ˈriəlɪ]		真的
mad [mæd]		生氣
awful [ˈɔfʊl]		形 很糟的；可怕的
accuse [əˈkjuz]		指控
jerk [dʒɝk]		無用的人；差勁的人
supervisor [supɚˈvaɪzɚ]		主管
necklace [ˈnɛklɪs]		項鍊
bet [bɛt]		動 打賭
stole [stol]		偷竊（steal的過去式）

Being Surprised

（驚訝）

 實用句型　　　　　　　　　　MP3-26

Oh my gosh!	我的天啊。
I don't believe it.	我真不敢相信。
He was shocked.	他真是嚇壞了。
I never would have guessed.	我怎麼也猜不到。

 開口說英語一

A: Boo!

（呼。）

B: Oh my gosh! I didn't see you there.

（我的天啊！我沒看到你在那裡。）

A: Did I scare you?

（我嚇著你嗎？）

B: You scared me half to death!

（你把我嚇得半死。）

A: Did you know that Mike is a singer?

（你知道邁可是個歌唱家嗎？）

B: No, I didn't.

（不知道。）

A: It's true. He even has a CD out and is planning to tour.

（是真的，他還出了光碟，正計畫要四處旅行演唱。）

B: Really? I'm shocked.
I never would have guessed.

（真的，我真是震驚，我從沒想到。）

單字

shock [ʃɑk]		震驚
guess [gɛs]		猜想
scare [skɛr]		使害怕
death [dɛθ]	名	死亡
tour [tʊr]		旅遊

Being Bored

（無聊）

MP3-27

I'm bored stiff.	我無聊死了。
He needs to get a hobby.	他需要找個嗜好。
I'm bored.	我好無聊。
I need to find something to do with myself.	我需要找事情做。
You've got too much time on your hands.	你手頭時間太多了。

A: I'm bored.

（我真的很無聊。）

B: Why don't you find something to do?

（你何不找一點事情做？）

A: I can't find anything.

（我找不到什麼事情做。）

B: You've got too much time on your hands. You need to get a hobby.

（你時間太多了，你需要找一個嗜好。）

A: How was class?

（上課上得怎麼樣？）

B: It was so lame. I was bored stiff.

（了無新意，我無聊死了。）

A: It couldn't have been that bad.

（不可能那麼糟的。）

B: Oh it was.

I could barely keep my eyes open.

（是那麼糟，我眼睛簡直張不開。）

bored [bord]	無聊的
stiff [stɪf]	僵硬的
hobby [ˈhɑbɪ]	嗜好
lame [lem]	落後於時代的
barely [ˈbɛrlɪ]	副 幾乎不能

Loneliness

（寂寞）

I'm lonely.	我很寂寞。
I hate to eat alone.	我不喜歡自己一個人吃飯。
He doesn't know anybody.	他不認識任何一個人。
She's never been alone before.	她以前沒有獨自一個人過。
I really miss him.	我真的很想念他。
He hates being by himself.	他不喜歡獨自一個人。

A: I appreciate you coming to dinner with me.

（我很感激你來跟我一起用餐。）

B: It was no problem really.

（這沒什麼。）

A: I just hate to eat alone.

（我就是不喜歡獨自一個人吃飯。）

B: I understand. Eating alone always makes me feel lonely.

（我知道，獨自一個人吃飯總是令我覺得孤單寂寞。）

開口說英語二

A: I heard that you and Jenny broke up.

（我聽說你跟珍妮兩人分手了。）

B: We did.

（是的。）

A: How are you doing?

（你還好吧？）

B: Actually, I've been pretty lonely. I didn't think I would, but I really miss her.

（事實上，我很孤單，我沒想到，但是我真的很想念她。）

lonely [ˈlonlɪ]	形	寂寞的；孤獨的
alone [əˈlon]	形	孤單的；單獨的
miss [mɪs]	動	想念
appreciate [əˈpriʃɪ,et]	動	感激
problem [ˈprɑbləm]		問題

Being Hungry

（肚子餓）

MP3-29

 實用句型

I'm starving!	我餓死了。
I could eat a horse.	我吃的下一匹馬。
I could die of starvation.	我會餓死。
He's starving to death.	他快餓死了。

 開口說英語一

A: What do you want for dinner?

（你晚餐要吃什麼？）

B: I don't care. I'm starving!

（什麼都可以，我快餓死了。）

A: Are you sure you don't care?

（真的什麼都可以？）

B: I'm so hungry right now.
I'll eat anything.

（我現在好餓，什麼都吃。）

A: I'm starving to death!

（我快餓死了。）

B: Me too.
What should we have for dinner?

（我也是，我們晚餐應該吃什麼？）

A: I don't know but we'd better have a lot of it.

（我不知道，但是我最好吃很多。）

B: I know.

I'm so hungry I could eat a horse.

（我知道，我好餓，可以吃得下一匹馬。）

單字

starving [ˈstɑrvɪŋ]		很餓
starvation [starˈveʃən]		飢餓
die [daɪ]		過世
care [kɛr]		在乎；在意

Being Tired

（疲倦的）

I'm beat!	我累壞了。
She's completely exhausted.	她完全累壞了。
You look run down.	你看起來很累的樣子。
I feel so worn out.	我覺得精疲力竭。
I'm drained.	我被榨乾了。
I think I'm about to pass out.	我想我快昏倒了。

開口說英語一

A: Are you okay? You look so run down.

（你好嗎？你看起來很累的樣子。）

B: I'm exhausted to tell you the truth.

（說真的，我真是累壞了。）

A: I guess you've had a pretty busy day.

（我猜你今天很忙。）

B: I sure have. Now I'm going to go home and pass out.

（是的，現在我要回家，倒頭就睡。）

開口說英語二

A: I feel so worn out.

（我覺得精疲力竭。）

B: Well, you have been pretty busy lately.

（你最近很忙。）

A: That's true, but I think I'm going to take some time off.

（是很忙，但是我就快請假休息了。）

B: I wish I could. I feel so drained.

（我希望我能休息，我覺得快被榨乾了。）

單字

beat [bit]	形	累壞了（形容詞）
drained [drend]		榨乾的
completely [kəmˈplitlɪ]		完全地
exhausted [ɪɡˈzɔstɪd]		筋疲力盡
pretty [ˈprɪtɪ]	副	非常；相當
true [tru]		真的

Feeling Uncomfortable

（覺得尷尬）

實用句型

He felt awkward asking her out.	要邀約她，他覺得很尷尬。
The way she stares at me makes me uncomfortable.	她凝視著我的樣子讓我很不安。
I don't like the way he looks at me.	我不喜歡他看著我的樣子。

開口說英語一

A: I hate asking someone out for a date.
（我不喜歡邀約人出去約會。）

B: I know what you mean. It's so awkward.
（我知道你的意思，那很尷尬的。）

A: I'm always worried that she'll say no.

（我總是會很擔心她會拒絕。）

B: Me too.　Asking people out makes me uncomfortable.

（我也是，邀約人出去約會令我不安。）

開口說英語二

A: My teacher makes me so uncomfortable.

（我的老師令我很不安。）

B: Really? Why is that?

（真的？為什麼？）

A: I don't know. Something about him just makes me squirm.

（我不知道，他就是令我跼促不安。）

B: Maybe you should take a different class. You may not learn very much if you stay in his.

（或許你應該上別的課，如果你留在他的班上，你不會學到任何東西。）

 單字

awkward [ˈɔkwɚd]		尷尬
stare [stɛr]		凝視
uncomfortable [ʌnˈkʌmfɚtəbl]		不自在；覺得尷尬
date [det]		約會
squirm [skwɝm]		踟促不安
stay [ste]		停留

Unit

12 **Being Scared**

（覺得害怕）

 實用句型

I'm scared.	我好怕。
I've never been so scared.	我沒有這麼害怕過。
He was afraid.	他很害怕。
You frightened me.	你嚇著我了。
I'm trembling.	我抖得很厲害。
She shook with fear.	她怕得發抖。
His heart was pounding.	他的心在碰碰跳。

A: Daddy, I'm scared.

（爹地，我好害怕。）

B: There's nothing to be afraid of.

（沒什麼好怕的。）

A: I know, but I'm still scared.

（我知道，但是我仍然害怕。）

B: Don't worry.

I'll leave the night light on.

（別擔心，我會把夜間燈開著。）

A: Oh! You frightened me.

（噢，你嚇了我一跳。）

B: I'm sorry I didn't mean to.

（很抱歉，我不是故意的。）

A: I guess I just didn't see you coming.

（我猜我只是沒看到你過來。）

B: You're trembling.

Did I really scare you that bad?

（你全身在發抖，我真的把你嚇得那麼厲害嗎？）

A: You sure did. My heart's pounding.

（確實是，我的心在碰碰跳。）

B: I really am sorry.

（我真的很抱歉。）

scared [skɛrd]		害怕的
afraid [əˈfred]		形 害怕
frighten [ˈfraɪtn̩]		動 使害怕
tremble [ˈtrɛmbl̩]		動 發抖
shook [ʃuk]		發抖（shake的過去式）
fear [fɪr]		名 動 害怕；憂慮
pound [paʊnd]		碰碰跳
guess [gɛs]		猜想
scare [skɛr]		使害怕

Unit

13 Feeling discouraged

（覺得挫折）

 實用句型   MP3-33

I quit.	我不做了。
I give up.	我放棄。
I'll never get it.	我得不到的。
I just can't do this.	我就是不會做。
This is too hard for me.	這對我來說太難了。

 開口說英語一

A: I quit. I just can't do this.

（我不做了，我就是不會做。）

B: Sure you can.

（你會的。）

A: No, I can't. It's just too hard for me.

（不，我不會，這對我來說太難了。）

B: Don't give up. I'll help you with it.

（別放棄，我會幫你的忙。）

A: I give up.

（我放棄了。）

B: What are you trying to do?

（你在嘗試做什麼？）

A: I'm trying to draw a cat but I'll never get it.

（我試著畫一隻貓，但是我畫不好的。）

B: Sure you will it just takes practice.

（你當然畫得好，只要你多練習。）

A: Will you show me how?

（你可以告訴我怎麼畫嗎？）

B: Of course. Hand me the paper.

（好的，把紙張給我。）

單字

quit [kwɪt]		辭職；終止
hard [hɑrd]		困難的
draw [drɔ]		畫
practice [ˈpræktɪs]		練習

Feeling guilty

（覺得內疚）

He felt so guilty.	我覺得很內疚。
I feel so bad about this.	關於這件事我覺得很難過。
It wasn't your fault.	那不是你的錯。
I'm the one to blame.	應該要怪我。
It was my fault.	是我的錯。
I feel terrible.	我難過極了。
I'm sorry I did that.	很抱歉我這麼做。
I didn't mean to hurt you.	我不是故意傷害你的。

There's no need to feel guilty.	沒必要覺得內救。
You're just feeling guilty.	你只是覺得內疚。

開口說英一

A: Tom left.
（湯姆離開了。）

B: Why?
（為什麼？）

A: He thinks you insulted him.
（他認為你侮辱了他。）

B: I feel so bad.
I didn't mean to hurt his feelings.
（我覺得很難過，我不是故意傷害他的感情。）

A: It's not your fault.

He's just too sensitive.

（那不是你的錯，他太敏感了。）

A: I'm sorry I broke your vase. I feel terrible about it.

（很抱歉我打破你的花瓶，我難過極了。）

B: Don't feel bad. It was an accident.

（別難過，是個意外。）

A: Still, I wish there was some way I could make it up to you.

（我希望有什麼方法我能夠補償。）

B: Don't worry about it.

I know you didn't do it on purpose.

（別擔心，我知道你不是故意的。）

單字

guilty	[ˈgɪltɪ]		內疚的
fault	[fɔlt]		過錯
blame	[blem]		歸罪於
terrible	[ˈtɛrəbl̩]	（口語）糟透的；可怕的	
hurt	[hɝt]		傷害
insult	[ɪnˈsʌlt]		侮辱
feelings	[ˈfilɪŋz]		人的感情
sensitive	[ˈsɛnsətɪv]		敏感的
vase	[ves]		花瓶
accident	[ˈæksədənt]		名 意外事件
on purpose			故意的

Unit 15

Feeling confused

（搞迷糊了）

I don't know what you want.	我不知道你要什麼。
What do you expect from me?	你期待我做什麼？
I'm confused.	我不知道該怎麼辦。
I don't understand.	我不了解。
He's just mixed up.	他只是搞錯了。
She's just confused about what she wants.	她只是搞不清楚她要什麼。

開口說英語一

A: Why didn't you do what I asked you to?

（你為什麼不照著我要你去做的做？）

B: I thought I did.

（我以為我是照你要求的做了。）

A: No, you got it all wrong.

（不是，你全搞錯了。）

B: I'm confused.

What do you expect from me?

（我不知道該怎麼辦，你期待我怎麼做？）

A: Are you planning to go to college?

（你計畫去上大學嗎？）

B: I'm not sure.

（我不確定。）

A: Well, what kind of job do you want to have?

（那，你想要什麼樣的工作？）

B: I don't know what I want.
I'm still trying to decide.

（我不知道我要什麼，我還在想辦法作決定。）

A: That is something you need to think about.

（那是你必須考慮的問題。）

B: You're right.

I have to make a decision soon.

（你說的對，我必須盡快做決定。）

 單字

expect [ɪk'spɛkt]		預期；期待
confused [kən'fjuzd]		形 弄糊塗了
understand [ˌʌndɚ'stænd]		瞭解；明白
wrong [rɔŋ]		錯誤的；出錯
college ['kɑlɪdʒ]		名 大學
job [dʒɑb]		工作；職位；職務
right [raɪt]		形 正確的
decision [dɪ'sɪʒən]		名 決定

Unit 16 **Disbelief**

（不相信）

實用句型

MP3-36

I don't believe it!	我不相信。
No way!	不可能的。
You're lying.	你在說謊。
How can that be?	怎麼可能？
That can't be true.	那不可能是真的。

開口說英語一

A: I'm sorry, John, but you flunked your exam.

（很遺憾，約翰，你考不及格。）

B: How can that be? I studied for days.

（怎麼可能？我勤讀好幾天的書。）

A: You must have studied the wrong thing.

（你一定讀錯東西了。）

B: I don't believe it. This is terrible.

（我不相信，這真是糟糕。）

A: There is a giant monster living under your bed.

（你的床底下有一隻巨大的怪物。）

B: No way! You're lying.

（不可能的，你在說謊。）

A: No, I'm not. There really is a monster under your bed.

（不，我沒有說謊，你的床底下真的有一隻怪物。）

B: But how can that be true? Dad says there are no such thing as monsters.

（但是，那怎麼可能是真的？爹地說沒有怪物這種東西。）

 單字

believe [brˈliv]		動 相信
flunk [flʌŋk]		（成績）當掉
exam [ɪgˈzæm]	考試（examination的縮寫）	
monster [ˈmɑnstɚ]		怪物

Unit 17 **Dislike**

（不喜歡）

實用句型

I don't like that very much.	我不太喜歡那個。
This is nasty.	這真是令人作嘔。
Yuck!	呸。
That's gross.	那真是噁心。
I really don't care for it.	我真的不喜歡。
I can't stand those things.	我不能忍受那些事情。

開口說英語一

A: Yuck! This is nasty!
（呸，真是令人作嘔。）

B: What is it?
（這是什麼？）

A: A peanut butter and tuna fish sandwich.
（花生醬和鮪魚醬三明治。）

B: That's gross! Why did you make that?
（那真噁心，你怎麼做這種三明治？）

A: I wanted to try something new.
（我想試試一些新的東西。）

A: What do you think of Jenny?

（你認為珍妮怎麼樣？）

B: To be honest, I don't like her very much.

（說老實話，我不太喜歡她。）

A: Why not?

（為什麼？）

B: She thinks she's better than everyone else.

（她認為她比其他每一個人都好。）

A: Really? I can't stand people like that!

（真的？，我受不了那樣的人。）

B: Me neither.

（我也受不了。）

單字

nasty [ˈnæstɪ]		令人討厭的；令人作嘔的
gross [gros]		（食物）令人噁心的
care [kɛr]		喜歡
sandwich [ˈsænwɪtʃ]		三明治
honest [ˈɑnəst]		誠實的

Showing approval

（表示贊同）

 實用句型

MP3-38

I like that a lot.	我很喜歡那個。
That one's my favorite.	那是我最喜歡的。
This is great!	這個真棒。
It's lovely.	這真可愛。
I think this one is best.	我認為這個是最好的。

 開口說英語一

A: That smells delicious.
（那聞起來真香。）

B: Thanks. I just made it.

（謝謝，我剛做的。）

A: Can I have a bite?

（我可以咬一口嗎？）

B: Sure. What do you think?

（當然可以，怎麼樣，好吃嗎？）

A: Yummy! I like that a lot.

（很好吃，我很喜歡。）

開口說英語二

A: Which picture should I hang in the living room?

（我應該把哪一張照片掛在客廳？）

B: Hang this one. I like it the best.

（掛這一張，我最喜歡這張。）

A: Really? I think this one is beautiful.

（真的？我覺得這張很漂亮。）

B: They're both beautiful but that one's my favorite.

（兩張都很漂亮，但是我最喜歡那張。）

favorite [ˈfevərɪt]		最喜歡的
lovely [ˈlʌvlɪ]	（口語）令人愉快的；美好的	
smell [smɛl]		動 聞到
delicious [dɪˈlɪʃəs]		形 好吃的；美味的
bite [baɪt]		名 一口
yummy [ˈʌmɪ]		好吃的
hang [hæŋ]		掛

Pride

（驕傲）

MP3-39

I was so proud when he won the award.	他得獎時我覺得很驕傲。
I'm really proud of my work.	我很以我的作品為傲。
Doing good deeds gave her a sense of pride.	做好事，讓她有自傲的感覺。
We're proud of you for trying so hard.	我們很以你的努力為傲。
Aren't you proud of him?	你不以他為榮嗎？

A: How was the awards ceremony?

（頒獎典禮進行的怎麼樣？）

B: My son got two awards for his art project.

（我兒子的藝術作品得了兩個獎。）

A: I bet you were thrilled.

（我打賭你一定樂壞了。）

B: I certainly was.

I've never been so proud.

（我是很高興，我從沒覺得這麼驕傲過。）

開口說英語二

A: My nephew broke my favorite glass.

（我姪兒把我最喜歡的玻璃杯打破了。）

B: How do you know he did it?

（你怎麼知道是他做的。）

A: He told me when it happened.

（事情發生時他就告訴我了。）

B: Aren't you proud of him for telling the truth?

（對於他說實話，你是否覺得很驕傲？）

A: Yes, I'm very proud of his honesty.

（是啊，我以他的誠實為傲。）

proud	[praʊd]	感到驕傲
award	[əˈwɔrd]	名 獎
deed	[did]	行為
pride	[praɪd]	名 驕傲
sense	[sɛns]	感覺
ceremony	[ˈsɛrəˌmonɪ]	名 典禮；儀式；慶典
project	[ˈprɑdʒɛkt]	企畫；學校研究作業
certainly	[ˈsɝtn̩lɪ]	當然；當然可以
glass	[glæs]	玻璃杯
nephew	[ˈnɛfju]	姪兒
truth	[truθ]	事實
honesty	[ˈɑnəstɪ]	誠實

Feeling Thirsty

（口渴）

MP3-40

I'm dying of thirst.	我快渴死了。
I'm so thirsty.	我好渴。
My throat is so dry.	我的喉嚨很乾。
Do you have anything to drink?	你有什麼可以喝嗎？
Can I get a drink?	有什麼飲料可以給我喝？
Would you like a drink?	你要喝飲料嗎？
What would you like to drink?	你要喝什麼？
What do you have to drink?	你有什麼飲料可以喝？

A: I'm so thirsty!

（我好渴。）

B: Would you like a drink?

（你要喝飲料嗎？）

A: That would be great.

（有飲料喝最好了。）

B: What would you like?

（你要喝什麼？）

A: Coke if you've got one.

（如果你有可樂的話，給我一瓶。）

B: One coke coming right up.

（我馬上拿瓶可樂給你。）

開口說英語二

A: I'm dying of thirst.

（我快渴死了。）

B: Me too. My throat is so dry.

（我也是，我的喉嚨很乾。）

A: We'll stop at the next store and get a drink.

（我們到下一個商店停下來，買個飲料。）

B: That'll be great.

I hope we get one soon.

（那很好，我希望很快買到飲料。）

單字

thirst [θɝst]	渴
throat [θrot]	喉嚨
drink [drɪŋk]	動 喝（飲料）；名 飲料
thirsty [ˈθɝstɪ]	渴的
next [nɛkst]	下一個

Chapter **3**

Things that people do

（事件）

Making Mistakes

（犯錯）

 實用句型

MP3-41

Oops!	糟了。
Oh man!	噢，天啊。
I didn't mean to.	我不是有意的。
It was an accident.	那是個意外。
It's all messed up.	全搞混了。
She made a big mistake.	她犯了一個大錯誤。
He really messed up this time.	這次他真是搞砸了。
I've really screwed this one up.	我真的把這件事搞砸了。

A: Oh man!

（噢，天啊。）

B: What happened?

（發生什麼事？）

A: I accidentally used the wrong color of paint. This picture's all messed up now.

（我不小心用錯了水彩顏色，這張圖完全是亂七八糟。）

B: Don't worry about it.

That one is just for practice.

（別擔心，這一張只是練習用。）

開口說英語二

A: Oh, no! I've made a big mistake.

（噢，不好，我犯了一個大錯誤。）

B: What did you do?

（你做了什麼？）

A: I told him that the meeting was at 2:00 instead of 12:00.

（我告訴他會議是兩點，而不是十二點。）

B: He's going to be so mad.
I hope he doesn't fire you.

（他一定會很生氣，我希望他別把你開除。）

A: But I didn't mean to tell him the wrong time.

（但是我不是故意跟他說錯誤的時間。）

B: I know, but this is the second time you've screwed up.

（我知道，但這是你第二次把事情搞砸。）

 單字

mean [min]		有意
accident ['æksədənt]	名	意外事件
mistake [mə'stek]	名	錯誤
screw [skru]		弄糟
accidentally [,æksə'dɛntl̩ɪ]	副	偶然地；意外地
wrong [rɔŋ]		錯誤的；出錯
paint [pent]		水彩
mess up		把…弄糟
practice ['præktɪs]		練習
fire [faɪr]	動	開除
second ['sɛkənd]		第二

Saying Goodbye

（說再見）

實用句型

Call me.	打電話給我。
Stop by sometime.	有空過來坐坐。
I'll be seeing you.	再見。
Don't be a stranger.	別好像陌生人一樣。
I'll see you around.	再見。

A: I'm late. I've got to go.

（已經遲了。我得走了。）

B: Well, it was nice talking to you again.

（很高興這次能再跟你聊天。）

A: Yeah, I'll see you around sometime.

（是啊，有空再見。）

B: Be sure to stop by once in a while.
Don't be such a stranger.

（有時一定要過來坐坐，別好像陌生人一樣。）

A: Are you leaving?

（你要離開了嗎？）

B: Yes, I've got to go.

（是的，我該走了。）

A: Give me a call next week.

（下星期給我打個電話。）

B: Okay, I'll be seeing you.

（好的，再見。）

單字

sometime	['sʌmtaɪm]	偶而
stranger	['strendʒɚ]	陌生人
late	[let]	遲到；很晚
again	[ə'gen]	再度；又

Unit 3

Looking for a Job

（找工作）

MP3-43

Do you know anyone who is hiring?	你知道有誰要雇用員工嗎？
I really need to find a new job.	我真的需要找一份新工作。
I'm ready to go to work.	我準備好可以上班了。
Do you know of anyone who needs some help?	你知不知道有誰需要幫手？
How's the job market?	就業市場情形怎麼樣？

A: I really need to find a new job.

（我真的需要找一份新的工作。）

B: I agree. It's time for you to get back to work.

（我贊同，也是你該重新就業的時候了。）

A: Do you know anyone who needs some help?

（你知不知道有誰需要幫手？）

B: I can't think of anyone but I'll ask around.

（我想不起有誰需要幫手，但是我可以問問看。）

開口說英語二

A: How's the job market?

（就業市場情形怎麼樣？）

B: It's tough. It took me two months to find
my job.

（很難，我花了兩個月才找到工作。）

A: Well, I'd better get busy looking.
I'm ready to go to work.

（那我可得用心一點找，我已準備好可以上班了。）

B: Just remember not to give up easily.
You'll find the right job.

（要記得別太容易放棄，你會找到適合的工作。）

單字

hire	[haɪr]		雇用
job	[dʒɑb]		工作；職位；職務
help	[hɛlp]		幫忙
market	[ˈmɑrkɪt]		市場
agree	[əˈgri]	動	同意
tough	[tʌf]		（口語）艱難
remember	[rɪˈmɛmbɚ]		記得

Forgetting

（忘記）

　實用句型　　　　　　　　　MP3-44

It must have slipped my mind.	我一定是忘了。
I didn't remember.	我不記得。
How could you forget that?	你怎麼可以忘記？
I forgot.	我忘了。

　開口說英語一

A: Did you remember to pick up my suit?
（你有沒有記得去拿我的套裝？）

B: Oh, no! It must have slipped my mind.

（噢，我一定是忘了。）

A: Now I don't have anything to wear tonight.

（我今晚沒有衣服可以穿了。）

B: Don't worry.

I still have time to go get it.

（別擔心，我還有時間去拿。）

開口說英語二

A: Tonight is our anniversary.

（今天是我們的週年紀念日。）

B: I don't believe that I forgot.

（我真不敢相信我竟忘了。）

A: How could you forget that?

（你怎麼可以忘記？）

B: I'm sorry.

I just didn't realize what day it was.

（對不起，我只是不知道今天是哪一天。）

slip	[slɪp]		滑
mind	[maɪnd]		頭腦
remember	[rɪˈmɛmbɚ]		記得
forget	[fɚˈgɛt]		忘記
forgot	[fɚˈgɑt]		忘記（forget的過去式）
wear	[wɛr]		動 穿；戴
anniversary	[ˌænəˈvɝsərɪ]		週年紀念日
realize	[ˈriəˌlaɪz]		明瞭；知道

Making Promises

（答應）

 實用句型

Don't make promises you can't keep.	你沒辦法達成的，就不要答應。
I can't promise anything.	我不能答應任何事。
He promised.	他答應了。
I promise to try my best.	我答應盡量。
A promise is a promise.	答應了就得遵守。

 開口說英語一

A: Will you take me to the circus on Saturday?

（你星期六要帶我去馬戲團嗎？）

B: I can't. I've got too much work to do.

（不行，我有太多事要做。）

A: But you promised!

（但是，你答應的。）

B: You're right, a promise is a promise.
We'll go to the circus on Saturday.

（你說的對，答應了就要遵守，我們星期六去看馬
戲團。）

開口說英語二

A: Can I have a new puppy?

（我可以有一隻小狗嗎？）

B: We'll see.

（再看看。）

A: Please!

I promise I'll never be bad again.

（拜託啦，我答應我會很乖。）

B: Don't make promises you can't keep.

（你做不到的事，不要隨便答應。）

 單字

promise [ˈprɑmɪs]		承諾；保證；答應
circus [ˈsɝkəs]		馬戲團
puppy [ˈpʌpɪ]		小狗
bad [bæd]		不好

MP3-46

Oh stop!	噢，停止這麼做。
Quit teasing me.	不要嘲笑我。
Stop pulling my leg.	別騙我。
You're always teasing.	你總是在嘲弄人。
Aren't you ever serious?	你不能正經一點嗎？
I'm just teasing you.	我只是在開玩笑。

開口說英語一

A: What's wrong?

（怎麼啦？）

B: You're being rude.

（你很無禮。）

A: I'm sorry, I'm just teasing you.

（對不起，我只是在開玩笑。）

B: You're always teasing.
Be serious for once.

（你總是在開玩笑，你就不能正經一次嗎？）

A: I just got a promotion.

（我升官了。）

B: Really?

（真的？）

That's great!

（那很棒。）

A: They've made me Vice President of the company.

（他們指定我當公司的副總裁。）

B: Stop pulling my leg. You've only been working there six months.

They'd never make anyone a vice president that soon.

（別騙我了，你才上班六個月，他們不可能這麼快升你當副總裁。）

 單字

quit [kwɪt]		辭職；終止
tease [tiz]		嘲笑；開玩笑
serious [ˈsɪrɪəs]		認真的；嚴肅的
rude [rud]		無禮的；魯莽的
once [wʌns]		一次
promotion [prəˈmoʃən]		升遷；晉級
company [ˈkʌmpənɪ]	名	公司
vice [vaɪs]		副的
president [ˈprɛzɪdənt]		總裁

Making plans to meet

（計畫見面）

Would you like to have dinner?	你要不要一起吃晚餐？
I'll meet you at the mall.	我會在購物中心跟你碰面。
I'll see you then.	到時再見。
What are you doing after school?	放學後你要做什麼？
I'll catch up with you later.	我稍候再跟你會合。

開口說英語一

A: What are you doing after work?
（你下班後要做什麼？）

B: I don't have any plans.
（我沒什麼計畫。）

A: Do you want to go to a movie?
（你要不要去看電影？）

B: That'd be cool but I need to go home first.
（很好，但是我需要先回家一趟。）

A: Okay, go home and then you can meet me later. I'll see you at the theater around 7:00.
（好的，你先回家，稍候你再跟我見面，我七點左右在戲院跟你見面。）

B: Great! I'll see you then.

（很好，再見。）

A: What are you going to do tonight?

（你今晚要做什麼？）

B: Nothing much, maybe go to the mall.

（沒什麼，或許到購物中心去。）

A: What time are you going?

（你什麼時候要去？）

B: Probably around 5:00.

（可能五點左右。）

A: How about I catch up with you then and we'll have dinner?

（我那時再來接你，我們一起去吃晚餐好嗎？）

B: Alright, I'll see you later.

（好的，再見。）

 單字

mall [mɔl]		大型購物中心
later ['letɚ]		稍後
plan [plæn]		計畫
movie ['muvɪ]		電影
theater ['θiətɚ]		戲院
tonight [tə'naɪt]		今晚
probably ['prɑbəblɪ]		或許；可能的

Choosing an activity

（選一個活動）

MP3-48

Let's go to swim.	我們去游泳。
I want to go dancing.	我要跳舞。
How about going to the zoo?	要不要去動物園？
I'd rather go fishing instead.	我寧願去釣魚。
Why don't we have a picnic?	我們何不去野餐？
How does shopping sound?	要不要去逛街？

A: What should we do this weekend?

（這個週末我們該做什麼？）

B: Why don't we go to the zoo?

（我們何不去動物園？）

A: I'd rather go dancing.

（我寧願去跳舞。）

B: Let's do both. We could go to the zoo in the afternoon and dancing at night.

（我們兩者都做，我們可以下午去動物園，晚上去跳舞。）

A: That sounds like a good plan.

（聽起來是個好計畫。）

A: Why don't we have a picnic tomorrow?

（我們明天去野餐怎麼樣？）

B: That would be fun but I heard it was going to rain.

（主意是不錯，但是我聽說會下雨。）

A: We could go shopping instead and have a picnic next week.

（我們可以去逛街，下星期再去野餐。）

B: That'll work out just fine.

（那很好。）

單字

zoo [zu]		動物園
picnic [ˈpɪknɪk]		野餐
sound [saʊnd]	動	聽起來
weekend [ˈwikˈɛnd]	名	週末

Getting lost

（迷路）

I don't know where I am.	我不知道我人在哪裡。
I think we're lost.	我想我們迷路了。
What should we do now?	我們現在怎麼辦？
Do you have a map?	你有地圖嗎？
What does the map say?	地圖怎麼說？
Let's take a left.	我們左轉。
Stop at the next gas station.	在加油站停。

開口說英語一

A: Oh no!

（噢，不好了。）

B: What's wrong?

（怎麼啦？）

A: I think we're lost.

I must have taken a wrong turn.

（我想我們迷路了，我一定是轉彎時轉錯了。）

B: What should we do now?

（我們現在怎麼辦？）

A: I think it would be best if we turned around.

（我想最好是轉回去。）

開口說英語二

A: Are we going the right way?

（我們是不是走錯路了？）

B: I'm not sure. What does the map say?

（我不太確定，地圖怎麼說？）

A: I'm sorry. I forgot to bring the map.

（對不起，我忘了帶地圖。）

B: Don't worry. We'll stop at that gas
station and ask directions.

（別擔心，我們在加油站停下來問路。）

單字

map [mæp]		地圖
left [lɛft]		左邊
station [ˈsteʃən]		車站；站；所；局
gas station		加油站
directions [dəˈrɛkʃənz]		方向指示

Unit

10 Asking for directions

（問路）

Do you know where to find the museum?	你知道怎麼找到博物館嗎？
Is this the way to the train station？	這是到火車站的路嗎？
Where is the Far East department store located?	遠東百貨公司在哪裡？
Am I headed in the right direction?	我走的方向對嗎？
Can you tell me how to get to the Central Park?	請告訴我如何到中央公園？
Could you give me directions to the train station?	請告訴我如何到火車站。

開口說英語一

A: Excuse me, do you know where to find the Hilton Hotel?

（對不起，請問到希爾頓飯店怎麼走？）

B: Yes, keep going straight and take a left at the third light.

（好的，你一直走，在第三個紅綠燈向左轉。）

A: A left at the third light?

（在第三個紅綠燈向左轉？）

B: That's it. The hotel will be on your right.

（是的，旅館就在你的右邊。）

A: Thanks for your help.

（謝謝你的幫忙。）

B: Don't mention it.

（別客氣。）

A: Can I help you?

（需要我幫忙嗎？）

B: Yes, I'm looking for the Central Park. Can you tell me if I'm headed in the right direction?

（是的，我在找中央公園，請告訴我，我走的方向對嗎？）

A: Actually, it looks like you got turned around.

You need to go back about half a mile.

（事實上，你走錯方向了，你需要往回走半哩路。）

B: Oh, I see. Thank you very much.

（噢，我知道了，謝謝。）

A: It was no problem at all.

（沒問題。）

單字

museum [mjuˈzɪəm]	博物館
department store	百貨公司
straight [stret]	直的
third [θɝd]	第三
mention [ˈmɛnʃən]	提起；談及

Unit 11

Breaking up

（分手）

MP3-51

I think it is over.	我想一切都過去了。
I don't want to date you anymore.	我不要再跟你約會了。
I need some space.	我需要一些空間。
You are way too serious.	你太認真了。
I'm not ready for this.	我還沒準備好。
I hope you're not upset.	我希望你不要生氣。
It's not working out.	我們合不來。

A: I need to talk to you.

（我需要跟你談談。）

B: About what?

（談什麼？）

A: I don't think we should date anymore.

You're way too serious.

I'm not ready for that.

（我認為我們不應該再繼續約會，你太認真了，我還沒準備好。）

B: I agree. Maybe we should break up.

（我同意，或許我們應該分手。）

A: I think it's time for us to break up.

（我想是我們分手的時候了。）

B: Why?

（為什麼？）

A: It's just not working out.

I need some space.

（我們之間合不來，我需要空間。）

B: Okay, if that's what you think.

（好的，如果你是這麼認為的話。）

A: I hope you're not upset.

（我希望你不要生氣。）

B: No, I'm fine. I'll see you around.

（不會，我很好，再見。）

單字

date	[det]	約會
space	[spes]	空間
serious	[ˈsɪrɪəs]	認真的
ready	[ˈrɛdɪ]	準備好
upset	[ˈʌpˈsɛt]	不高興

Entering a Contest

（參加比賽）

實用句型

I've decided to enter a writing contest.	我已經決定要參加寫作比賽。
Did you hear about the cooking contest?	你有沒有聽說烹飪比賽的事？
Why don't you enter that contest?	你為什麼不參加比賽？
You should enter it.	你應該參加。
I bet you'd have a good chance of winning.	我敢說你贏的機會很大。
There is a contest I think you should enter.	有一個比賽，我認為你應該參加。
I hope I win.	我希望我會贏。

Let's give it a shot.	我們來試試看。
You don't know if you don't try.	如果你沒有試，你不會知道。
The first prize is a trip to France.	頭獎是到法國旅遊。

開口說英語一

A: I've decided to enter a writing contest.

（我已經決定參加寫作比賽。）

B: Really? What can you win?

（真的？獎品是什麼？）

A: First prize is a trip to France.

（頭獎是到法國旅遊。）

B: That sounds great! What are you going to send in?

（聽起來很棒，你打算用什麼來參賽？）

A: I have a short story I've been working on.

（我一直在寫一篇短篇故事。）

B: Well, good luck.

（好吧，祝你好運。）

 開口說英語二

A: Did you hear about the cooking contest?

（你有沒有聽說烹飪比賽？）

B: No, I haven't.

（沒有。）

A: They are looking for the best cake in the city. I bet you'd have a good chance of winning.

（他們在找本市做的最好吃的蛋糕，我敢說你贏的機會很大。）

B: Oh, I don't know.

（噢，這我可不敢說。）

A: Why don't you enter it?

You don't know if you don't try.

（你何不參賽？如果你不參加，你不會知道。）

B: You're right. I'll give it a shot.

（你說的對，我會試試看。）

enter [ˈɛntɚ]		參賽
contest [ˈkɑntɛst]	名	競爭；比賽
win [wɪn]		贏
prize [praɪz]		獎品

Unit 13

Reading a Book

（看一本書）

I'm reading the best book right now.	我在看一本最好的書。
What book are you reading?	你在看什麼書？
Have you ever read Harry Potter?	你有沒有看過『哈利波特』這本書？
What do you think of that book?	你認為那本書怎麼樣？
You should really read this book.	你真的應該讀這本書。

開口說英語一

A: I'm reading the best book right now.

（我正在讀一本最好的書。）

B: Really! What's it called?

（真的？書名是什麼？）

A: The Count of Monte Cristo.
It's by Alexandre Dumas.

（基度山恩仇記，亞歷山大·仲馬寫的）

B: I've never heard of it.

（我沒聽說過這本書。）

A: You really should read it sometime.

（你有空應該要看。）

B: Thanks for telling me about it.
I'll have to check it out.

（謝謝你告訴我，我必須看看。）

開口說英語二

A: What are you reading?

（你在看什麼？）

B: Dracula. It's a great book.

（吸血鬼，是一本好書。）

A: I really liked it, too.

Have you ever read Frankenstein?

（我也真的很喜歡，你有沒有看過「科學怪人」？）

B: No, but I know you did.

What did you think of it?

（沒有，但是我知道你看過了，你認為怎麼樣？）

A: I think you'll like it.

（我想你會喜歡。）

B: Maybe I'll read it next.

（或許下一本我會讀那本書。）

單字

best	[bɛst]	最好的
really	[ˈriəlɪ]	真的
should	[ʃʊd]	應該
next	[nɛkst]	下一個

Making Something

（做東西）

MP3-54

I'm making something for my father.	我在做東西給我爸爸。
What are you making?	你在做什麼？
I'm making a pair of pajamas.	我在做一件睡衣。
Did you make this?	這是你做的嗎？
Making jewelry is my hobby.	做珠寶是我的興趣。
I really like the picture you made.	我很喜歡你做的圖。

開口說英語一

A: What are you getting mom for her birthday?

（你要買什麼給媽當生日禮物？）

B: I'm going to make her something.

（我想做東西給她。）

A: She really liked that robe you made.

（她很喜歡你做的袍子。）

B: Maybe I will make her some pajamas this time.

（或許這次我會做睡衣給她。）

開口說英語二

A: Where did you get that ring?

（那個戒子你哪裡買的？）

B: I made it.

Making jewelry is my hobby.

（我做的，做珠寶是我的興趣。）

A: Did you make that necklace, too?

（那條項鍊也是你做的嗎？）

B: Yes, but my friend gave me this bracelet.

（是的，但是這個手鐲是我朋友給我的。）

單字

pajamas	[pəˈdʒæməs]	睡衣
hobby	[ˈhɑbɪ]	嗜好
picture	[ˈpɪktʃɚ]	圖畫
robe	[rob]	袍子
jewelry	[ˈdʒuəlrɪ]	珠寶
bracelet	[ˈbreslɪt]	手鐲

Using the Phone

（使用電話）

Hold on a second, I'm on the phone.	稍候，我正在講電話。
Who's on the phone?	是誰在講電話？
I need to use the phone real quick.	我急需用電話。
May I use the phone?	我可以用電話嗎？
Wait until I'm off the phone.	等我用完電話。
I can't pay attention to you.	我沒空聽你說話。
I'm on the phone.	我在講電話。

I'll be off in a minute.	我一下子就講完了。

開口說英語一

A: Can I ask you something?
（我可以問你個問題嗎？）

B: Hold on a second. I'm on the phone.
（稍候，我在講電話。）

A: Will you be on long?
（你會講很久嗎？）

B: No, I'll be off in just a minute.
（不會，我一下子就講完了。）

A: Okay, then.
I'll wait until you're through.
（好的，我等你講完。）

開口說英語二

A: Who's on the phone?

（誰在講電話？）

B: I am. Why?

（是我，有什麼事嗎？）

A: I need to use the phone real quick.

（我急需用電話。）

B: Okay, I'll get off. But it's going to be a minute. They've put me on hold.

（對方要我稍候，好的，我盡快掛斷，但是，要等幾分鐘。）

A: Thanks. Will you let me know when you're off?

（謝謝，你電話掛斷之後，跟我說一聲。）

B: Sure. I'll come and get you.

（好的，我會來找你。）

second [ˈsɛkənd]		片刻
quick [kwɪk]	形	快的；迅速的
attention [əˈtɛnʃən]	名	注意
through [θru]		完成的；結束的

Unit 16

Doing Homework

（做家庭作業）

When is this paper due?	這個報告什麼時候要交？
Do you want to study together?	你要不要一起唸書？
Maybe we can do our homework together.	或許我們可以一起做功課。
Aren't you in my group?	你不是在我那一組嗎？
I'll do problems one through fifteen.	我做第一題到第十五題。
You do problem seven.	你做第七題。

A: Aren't you in my group at school?

（你不是在我那一組嗎？）

B: Yes, we have English Literature together.

（是的，我們一起做英國文學。）

A: Do you know when that paper is due?

（你知道那篇報告什麼時候要交嗎？）

B: On the fifteenth.

The exam is on the twentieth.

（十五號，考試是二十號。）

A: Do you think we could study together?

（你想我們可以一起讀書嗎？）

B: I'd like that. Why don't we get together this weekend?

（我喜歡一起讀，我們何不這個週末一起讀？）

開口說英語二

A: I'm having trouble in my science class.

（我在科學課有困難。）

B: Me too.

Maybe we should study together.

（我也是，或許我們可以一起讀。）

A: That's not a bad idea.

Are you free tonight?

（那是個不錯的主意，你今晚有空嗎？）

B: Yes. Meet me at the library around eight o'clock.

（有，八點左右在圖書館等我。）

單字

paper	['pepɚ]		研究報告
due	[dju]		期限截止
homework	['hom'wɝk]		家庭作業
group	[grup]		名 群；團體
through	[θru]	介 從~到	形 完成的；結束的
science	['saɪəns]		科學
library	['laɪˌbrɛrɪ]		名 圖書館

Unit

17 Moving

（搬家）

I'm thinking about moving.	我在考慮搬家。
I'd like to get a bigger place.	我想找個大一點的地方。
I've only got three days left to pack.	我只有三天可以打包。
We're moving closer to my work.	我們要搬到靠近我工作的地方。
She will be moving in the fall.	她秋天要搬家。

 開口說英語一

A: I'm thinking about moving.

（我在考慮搬家。）

225

B: Why? Don't you like it here?

（為什麼？你不喜歡這裡嗎？）

A: It's okay but I'd like to get a bigger place.

（這裡還好，但是我喜歡大一點的地方。）

B: Are you sure that's a good idea?
What if you can't make the rent?

（你確定那是麼好主意嗎？如果你繳不起房租呢？）

A: I'm not worried. I just got a new job.

（我不擔心。我剛找到一個新工作。）

開口說英語二

A: When do you plan on moving?

（你計畫什麼時候搬家？）

B: We're looking at a house right now.
It's closer to my work.

（我們現在在看一間房子，距離我上班的地方較近。）

A: That will be nice.

（那很好。）

B: I know. I can't wait to move into it!

（我知道，我等不及搬進去。）

 單字

pack [pæk]		裝箱
fall [fɔl]		秋天
move [muv]		搬家
rent [rɛnt]		租金

Unit 18 **Playing Games**

（玩遊戲）

Do you want to play basketball?	你要不要打籃球？
Whose turn is it?	輪到誰？
It's my turn	輪到我。
What game are you playing?	你們在玩什麼遊戲？
Let's play something else.	我們來玩其他的遊戲。
How many people can play that game?	那個遊戲多少人可以玩？

A: What are you doing?

（你們在做什麼？）

B: We're playing a game.

Do you want to play, too?

（我們在玩遊戲，你也要玩嗎？）

A: What are you playing?

（你們在玩什麼？）

B: It's called Monopoly.

（大富翁。）

A: I guess it won't hurt to try it.

（我想試試也無妨。）

B: No, you'll like it. It's a lot of fun.

（你一定會喜歡的，很好玩的。）

開口說英語二

A: Whose turn is it?

（輪到誰？）

B: It's my turn.

（輪到我。）

A: I thought you just went.

（我以為你剛玩過。）

B: No, Mary just went.
I haven't gone yet.

（不是，瑪麗剛玩過，我還沒玩。）

A: Whose turn is it after you?

（在你之後輪到誰？）

B: After me, it's your turn.

（在我之後，輪到你。）

basketball	[ˈbæskɪtˌbɔl]	名 籃球
turn	[tɝn]	輪流
game	[gem]	（球類）比賽；遊戲
fun	[fʌn]	好玩；樂趣
yet	[jɛt]	副 尚未

Taking a Walk

（散步）

Do you want to go for a walk?	你要不要去散步？
Let's take a walk.	我們去散散步。
I think I'm going to take a walk.	我想我要去散散步。
It's nice out here.	出來這裡真好。
Get a jacket.	拿一件夾克。
He likes to walk every evening.	他喜歡每天傍晚散步。
She's going for her afternoon walk.	她去做午後散步。

A: Where's he going?
（他去哪裡？）

B: He's going for his afternoon walk.
（他去做午後散步。）

A: That sounds like a good idea.
Do you want to go for a walk?
（聽起來是個好主意，你要去散散步嗎？）

B: Sure. Let me get my jacket.
（好的，我去拿件夾克。）

A: It's nice out here. I think I'll take a walk.
（出來這裡真好，我想我要去散散步。）

B: I like to take a little walk every evening.
I enjoy the night air.

（我喜歡每天傍晚散散步，我喜歡晚上的空氣。）

A: Then why don't you come, too?

（那你何不一起來？）

B: Thanks, I think I will.

（謝謝，我想我一起來散步好了。）

單字

jacket [ˈdʒækɪt]		夾克；外套
air [ɛr]		空氣

Taking a Cab

（搭計程車）

Taxi!	計程車。
51st and Main Street please.	請開到第五十一街和緬因街。
How much is the fare?	車費是多少？
Do you have change for a twenty?	二十塊錢你找得開嗎？
The Hilton Hotel, please.	請開到希爾頓飯店。
Shall we share a cab?	我們一起搭計程車好嗎？

A: Taxi!

（計程車。）

B: Where you headed?

（你要去哪裡？）

A: The Hilton Hotel, please.

（請開到希爾頓飯店。）

B: No problem.

（沒問題。）

A: I need to catch a cab.

（我需要叫部計程車。）

B: So do I. Where are you going?

（我也是，你要去哪裡？）

A: To 17th and St. Louis.

（到第十七街和聖路易街。）

B: I'm headed that way, too.

Maybe we should share a cab.

（我也是往那個方向，或許我們可以共搭一部計程車。）

A: That'd be great. We could split the fare.

（那很好，我們可以均攤計程車費。）

單字

taxi [ˈtæksɪ]		計程車
fare [fɛr]		車資
change [tʃendʒ]	名 零錢；小額硬幣	
cab [kæb]		計程車
catch [kætʃ]		趕上
split [splɪt]		均攤

Unit

21 Making an Order on the Phone

（用電話訂購）

 實用句型

I would like to order a microwave.	我要訂購一個微波爐。
I need two of those.	我需要兩個。
Does that item come in blue?	那個物品有藍色的嗎？
When will that be available?	什麼時候會有貨？
Is overnight shipping extra?	如果隔夜快遞要加價嗎？
When can I expect my order to arrive?	我訂購的東西什麼時候會到？

A: Thank you for calling Sears.
How can I help you?

（謝謝你打電話來席爾斯百貨公司。需要什麼幫忙嗎？）

B: Yes, I'd like to make an order from your catalog.

（我要訂購你們目錄上的貨品。）

A: Alright, what would you like?

（好的，你要什麼？）

B: I'd like the Midnight dress on page 17.
It's item #2555.

（我要目錄上第十七頁的晚禮服，項目號碼是二五五五號。）

A: What else can I get for you today?

（還需要什麼其他的東西嗎？）

B: That should do it for now.

（今天訂購這件就好。）

開口說英語二

A: Your total comes to $183.00.

（總價是一百八十三元。）

B: When can I expect my shipment to arrive?

（什麼時候，貨會到？）

A: It should be there in three to five days.

（應該要三到五天。）

B: How much extra is overnight shipping?

（隔夜快遞要多付多少錢？）

A: $12.00.

（十二元。）

B: I'd like to have it sent overnight.

（請你用隔夜快遞。）

A: No problem, sir.

Your new total is $195.00.

（好的，新的總價是一百九十五元。）

單字

microwave	[ˈmaɪkrəˌwev]	微波爐
item	[ˈaɪtəm]	貨品；項目
available	[əˈveləbl̩]	有得賣的；可得的
extra	[ˈɛkstrə]	額外的；多餘的
overnight	[ˌovɚˈnaɪt]	隔夜
expect	[ɪkˈspɛkt]	預期；期待
arrive	[əˈraɪv]	動 抵達
catalog	[ˈkætl̩ˌɔg]	目錄

Asking for Advice

（問建議）

What should I do?	我該做什麼？
I need some advice.	我需要一些建議。
What do you think?	你認為怎麼樣？
What's your opinion?	你的意見如何？
That sounds like a good idea.	聽起來是個好主意。
I'm just not sure.	我不確定。
I don't know what to do.	我不知道該怎麼做。

A: I need some advice.

（我需要一些建議。）

B: What's the problem?

（有什麼問題？）

A: I'm not sure if I should take that new job.

（我不確定是否該接那個新工作？）

B: Well, it sounds like it offers some good benefits.

But, you're happy at your old job.

（聽起來這個工作的福利較好，但是，你的舊工作你做得很愉快。）

A: What should I do?

（我該怎麼辦？）

B: I'm just not sure. Why don't you ask your father's opinion?

（我不確定，你何不問你父親的意見？）

開口說英語二

A: I don't know what to do, Mary.

（瑪麗，我不知道該怎麼做。）

B: What do you mean?

（你是什麼意思？）

A: Should I break up with John or give him another chance?

（我應該跟約翰分手或是再給他一個機會？）

B: That's something you need to decide for yourself.

（那是你自己必須決定的事？）

advice [ədˈvaɪs]		忠言；勸告；建議
opinion [əˈpɪnjən]		意見
idea [aɪˈdɪə]		主意；概念
sure [ʃʊr]	形	的確的；確定；毫無疑問的
problem [ˈprɑbləm]		問題
benefit [ˈbɛnəfɪt]	名	福利
chance [tʃæns]	名	機會
another [əˈnʌðɚ]		另一個
break up		分手
decide [dɪˈsaɪd]	動	決定
yourself [jʊrˈsɛlf]		你自己

Giving Advice

（忠告）

 實用句型

In my opinion you should quit smoking.	依我的意見，你應該戒煙。
Take my advice.	接受我的建議。
All I can do is offer my advice.	我所能做的就是給你我的建議。
I think you should tell him the truth..	我認為你應該跟他說實話。
I'm only telling you what I think is best for you.	我只是跟你說我認為對你最好的。

 開口說英語一

A: I really want to go shopping.

（我真的想要去購物。）

B: That would be fun but we have bills to pay.

（去購物是很好玩，但是我們有很多帳單要付。）

A: I could go shopping and pay my bills next week.

（我可以去購物，下星期再付帳單。）

B: Take my advice.

Pay the bills now and shop later.

（接受我的建議吧。先付帳單，然後再購物。）

開口說英語二

A: I'm not sure I want to stay with Julie.

（我不確定我想繼續跟朱莉在一起。）

B: To be honest, I don't think you should.

（老實說，我不認為你應該跟她在一起。）

A: You're just saying that because you don't like her.

（你這麼說，因為你不喜歡她。）

B: I like Julie a lot.

I'm only telling you what I think is best for you.

（我很喜歡朱莉，我只是跟你說我認為對你最好的。）

 單字

should [ʃʊd]		應該
quit [kwɪt]		終止
truth [truθ]		事實
pay [pe]		付錢
bill [bɪl]	图	帳單

Unit 24 Taking a Vote

（投票）

實用句型

MP3-64

Let's vote on it.	讓我們投票決定。
We should take a vote.	我們應該投票。
Who votes yes?	誰贊成？
All in favor, raise your hand.	贊成的，舉手。
All who agree raise your hand.	所有贊成的請舉手。
Does any one oppose?	有沒有人反對？
Shall we take a vote?	我們應該投票嗎？

A: I'm trying to make a fair decision.

（我正試著做一個公平的決定。）

B: Let's vote on it.

（我們投票好了。）

A: That's a good idea. Then we'll know how everyone feels about it.

（那是個好主意，那樣我們就知道大家的想法。）

B: Great. All in favor, raise your hand.

（很好，贊成的，請舉手。）

A: How can we decide if we should raise the price?

（我們怎麼決定，我們是否應該提高價格？）

B: Shall we take a vote?

（我們應該投票決定嗎？）

A: Fine.

（好的。）

B: Should we raise the price of this toy? Who votes yes? Does any one oppose?

（這個玩具我們應該提高價格嗎？誰贊成？有沒有人反對？）

單字

vote [vot]		投票
raise [rez]	動	提高
oppose [ə'poz]	動	反對
decision [dɪ'sɪʒən]	名	決定

Inviting Someone to an Event

（邀請）

MP3-65

I'd love it if you would come.	如果你能來我會很高興。
Would you care to come?	你會來嗎？
I hope to see you there.	我希望在那裡看到你。
It would mean a lot to me if you came.	如果你能來，對我意義很重大。
I hope you can make it.	我希望你能來。

A: Sam's paintings are going to be in the museum.

（山姆的油畫將會在博物館展出。）

B: That's wonderful!

（那很棒。）

A: The opening is at 7:30 tonight if you'd like to come.

（如果你想來的話，今晚七點半開幕。）

B: I'd love to.
Tell Sam I'll try my best to make it.

（我想來，跟山姆說我會儘量趕來。）

A: Great. Hope to see you there.

（很好，希望在那裡看到你。）

開口說英語二

A: I'm going to get an award next week.
（我下星期會得到一個獎。）

B: Congratulations!
（恭喜。）

A: There's going to be a dinner afterwards.
It would mean a lot to me if you came.
（頒獎之後會有一個晚餐會，如果你能來，對我的意義很大。）

B: I'd love to go.
（我想去。）

Thanks for inviting me.
（謝謝你邀請我。）

mean [min]		意義
painting ['pentɪŋ]		圖畫
museum [mju'zɪəm]		博物館
opening ['opənɪŋ]		開幕
congratulations [kən,grætʃə'leʃənz]		恭喜
invite [ɪn'vaɪt]		邀請

國家圖書館出版品預行編目資料

輕鬆學會美語會話/蘇盈盈著. -- 新北市：哈福
企業有限公司, 2021.07
　面；　公分. --（英語系列；73）

ISBN 978-986-06114-4-1(平裝附光碟片)

1.英語 2.會話

805.188　　　　　　　　　　110010261

英語系列：73

....

書名/ **輕鬆學會美語會話**
作者 / 蘇盈盈
出版單位 / 哈福企業有限公司
責任編輯 / Judy Wu
封面設計 / Lin Lin House
內文排版 / Co Co
出版者 / 哈福企業有限公司
地址 / 新北市板橋區五權街 16 號 1 樓

....

電話／ (02) 2808-4587
傳真／ (02) 2808-6545
郵政劃撥／ 31598840
戶名/哈福企業有限公司
出版日期／ 2021 年 7 月
定價／ NT$ 330 元（附 MP3）
港幣定價／ 110 元（附 MP3）

....

全球華文國際市場總代理／采舍國際有限公司
地址／新北市中和區中山路 2 段 366 巷 10 號 3 樓
電話／ (02) 8245-8786 傳真／ (02) 8245-8718
網址／ www.silkbook.com 新絲路華文網

....

香港澳門總經銷／和平圖書有限公司
地址／香港柴灣嘉業街 12 號百樂門大廈 17 樓
電話／ (852) 2804-6687 傳真／ (852) 2804-6409

....

email ／ welike8686@Gmail.com
網址／ Haa-net.com
facebook ／ Haa-net 哈福網路商城
Original Copyright © AA Bridgers, Inc. USA

....